A Killer Cut

By

M.K. Stabley

This book is a work of fiction. Names, characters, places, and incidents are either the product of the author's imagination, or are used fictitiously. Any resemblance to actual persons or events is entirely coincidental.

This book is dedicated to the amazing women I worked with at Green Door Salon. They made every day a true adventure. We had fun, we had crazy, and we had sadness. But, I wouldn't change it for anything. I love each and every one of you.

And to my husband and son, thank you for putting up with my writing aspirations and dreams. I couldn't have finished this book without you both. I love you both to the moon and back. Always and Forever.

Chapter 1

The sound of blow dryers and gossip abound today throughout the busiest salon in town. "Oh my God Lucy, did you see the outfit Margie had on today, she looked like a rolled pork loin," is just some of what is heard among the noise.

A Cut Above Salon and Spa, is located in the quaint little town of Delaware, Ohio. Delaware is one of the fastest growing suburbs in the US, and its downtown area is super cute, with its hundred year old brick buildings, that once housed general stores and old saloons, now host loads of shops restaurants, bars, wineries, banks and law offices, as well as loft apartments on the upper floors. A Private University is downtown, also, so college kids galore, are roaming the downtown area, all the time.

The site where A Cut Above is located, is over a hundred years old, and has the same hardwood floors it had in it from 1890. It is decorated in rustic chic decor with lots of handmade accents and barn doors separating rooms, and electric and plumbing from the 19th Century. Depending on how many dryers are going at once, a breaker could go.

Eva St.Claire, the manager and receptionist at the salon looks on at all that is going on around the main floor, and smiles. It entertains her, thoroughly. Eva is in her late forties, always has a bright white smile, and her makeup is always tastefully done. She has blond shoulder length highlighted hair, and dresses trendy, even for her petite and very curvy figure.

The girls are all highly talented, and are all like family. The clients, they are all types. Some as sweet as pie, others, rude as hell and have zero patience. One in particular, seems to stand out, and here she comes now, in her Donna Karen pant suit, Jimmy Choo shoes, and Louie Vuitton handbag.

"Good Morning, Trudy." Eva greeted her, with a big jovial smile. "Can I get you anything to drink, while Chrissy is finishing up?

"Coffee, with cream, and no sugar", she says, with a curtness in her voice.

While Eva was getting her coffee, she looked toward Chrissy. She looked up, smiled and rolled her eyes to the sky, she knew who was there. They both smiled, as they shared their little private entertaining conversation.

"Here is your coffee Mrs. Marshall." Silence...

Yep, just like always; no thank you, no nothing.

Eva was used to that with her, and she didn't let it bother her.

She knew all too well, about Trudy Marshall. She was in her fifties, average height, slender build, had silver streaks in her hair that framed her thin, overly botoxed face. She was married to none other than Troy Baylor, one of the richest men in town. He made his money selling expensive farming equipment, and horse training.

He was famous for his winning horses. Mr. Baylor was also on every Board of Directors seats that you could think of, including the city planning committee. He was 75 years old, but looked like he was 90, and he was a stingy bastard. Trudy obviously married him for his money, because it sure wasn't for his looks or his gracious heart. He has two daughters from his first marriage. His first wife has been deceased for fifteen years now, and the daughters hate Trudy with a passion.

Trudy sees Chrissy every Friday, at 10am, without fail. She followed Chrissy from the salon she previously worked at, The Bold and Beautiful Salon, or as they call it, The B&B Salon, for short. The owner, Alice Bertrum, used to do Trudy's hair, before Chrissy came along. Once she met Chrissy, she hasn't gone back. Alice has never gotten over that. One thing you never do to a hairdresser is steal her clients, especially one as rich and powerful as Trudy Marshall.

All the girls that are at A Cut Above Salon, used to work at the B&B, before leaving to work for Chrissy, Shannon, Sarah, and Chelsea. It'll be 1 year this Christmas that they have been in business, and business is booming. They did, however, leave the other salon on not so good terms, and took 90% of their clients with them, and they've never looked backed.

Both salons are located in the downtown area, only a block away from each other. Alice's son, Gerard has been known to harass the girls on the street, if he sees them near his salon. A lot of animosity there, for sure.

Eva was constantly on her feet, walking from the front to the back of the salon, at least a hundred times or more a day. She saw everything that was going on, heard everything being said, not that anyone was whispering, but she did hear quite a lot of trash throughout the day. Most of it, she tried ignoring or tuned it out. Going home at the end of the day to her husband and boys, made her appreciate what a quiet and normal life she actually led.

"Eve! How much longer am I going to have to sit here and wait for Chrissy," Trudy yelled out loud, for all to hear. Even calling her by the wrong name, made all the girls look up in question.

Chrissy looked up, appalled by the comment. She looked at Eva, to see how she would respond, and hoped she would keep her calm, and not blow her top.

Eva made eye contact with Chrissy, nodded and turned her attention back to Mrs. Marshall, and said in her sweet voice, "it looks like she is just finishing up with her client now, so it shouldn't be but a couple minutes."

"Well, this is inconvenient. I made an appointment for 10am, I expect to be sitting in that chair by 10am, if not a minute sooner."

Eva glanced rather quickly at the clock, it had just turned 10am, on the dot. She could feel her eyes roll, and had to stop herself. She looked back at Chrissy, who was finishing with her client, but had quite a smirk on her face, too. She had to have seen what Eva did.

As Chrissy was walking her finished client to the front desk to check out, she was all smiles and wasn't going to let the incident ruin her morning.

"Eva, can you please ring Shirley out, she was a cut and color, today. Thanks for coming in, Shirley. Okay Mrs. Marshall, I am sorry for the delay, let's get you back here, shall we," Chrissy said, nonchalantly.

"You know Chrissy if you can't get me in on time, I may have to go back to Alice, I am sure she wouldn't make me wait," she threatened, in her snooty tone.

"Maybe she wouldn't, but I have apologized, and I am going to do my best to keep you satisfied, Trudy, but if you feel I can no longer serve you properly, then by all means, do what you feel is necessary. And by the way, her name is Eva, not Eve."

All went quiet in the salon for those few seconds, then Trudy was speechless, not something that happens very often. She sat in her chair, and never said another word. The loud dryers, washbasins, chatter and normalcy returned.

The rest of the day was pretty typical, a constant stream of women, children and even a few men came in and went out, with new dos or pretty nails. They do relaxation massage and facials, too. For the most part though, it's all about the hair.

Chapter 2

Emma Walker, one of the best colorists they have, walked in all smiles and looked proud. Emma is in her mid-thirties, blond shoulder-length hair with a bright blue streak on the one side, petite in stature, not overly skinny, but pretty. She is a mother to four girls. She is divorced and has had her share of loser dates, but keeps trucking along.

"Hey bitches, what's up?"

"Emma, could you be anymore vulgar," Shannon yelled.

"Actually yes, I could be but I won't."

Shannon laughed at her brutal honesty. Shannon is such a sweet, innocent woman. She couldn't hurt a fly, even if she wanted to. She'd invite it to bite her just so it wouldn't feel bad. Being that she is one of the owners of the salon, and loved by all her clients. She always tries to cater to their needs. Chrissy has been voted "Best Stylist" a few years running in the local paper. Shannon is a cute, petite redhead with two grown boys, and has been happily married forever.

"Emma, why are you all smiles, today? Did you finally get laid, honey?"

Everyone in ear shot nearly choked when they looked up to see who said that. Shannon never says those kinds of words. She was laughing herself at what she'd just blurted out.

"Geeze Shannon, what the hell? No, I didn't get laid. But, I did hear some juice coming out of here. I heard of the little outburst Trudy Marshall had earlier. You really gave her a what for, didn't you Chrissy?"

Chrissy tried to look embarrassed. The reality was, she was proud of herself for standing up to Trudy.

"That woman drives me crazy. I've dreamed of taking scissors to her on many occasions. It's no wonder I have homicidal tendencies."

"Don't let anyone else hear you say that," Sarah chimed in.

"Oh please Sarah, you can't tell me you have never fanaticized about doing something horrible to one of your worst clients."

"Of course, but I would never say it out loud."

Sarah would definitely say it loud. She never keeps a thought in her head. She is quite outspoken. She has also been a stylist the longest, about 30 years. Sarah is in her late forties, shoulder length brunette hair, average height, heavier, but kicking some diet butt, before she goes on her dream vacation. She is one of the owners of the salon, as well.

Having four owners all being women, it could get pretty dicey at times and chaotic. One never knows what the other is doing. That's where Eva usually steps in and takes over the organization part, or at least trying to keep order in an otherwise disorganized environment. Eva was looking at the clock and realized it was about time to go home.

"Goodnight girls, see you in the morning," Eva waved, as she left the shop.

Chapter 3

After Chrissy left the shop, she truly didn't feel like going home, she headed to the barn to see her horse. She was her stress reliever. Muffin loved her, and in turn Chrissy treated her like family. The barn was the source of her solace. She loved it there. It was quiet and peaceful. Tonight, no one was there.

As she walked into the barn Muffin walked over to her, put her nose into Chrissy's chest and let her stroke her mane. Muffin was a beautiful American Quarter Horse with a shiny brown color and a black mane and tail. Muffin was strong, absolutely stunning to watch, and so friendly.

"Oh Muffin, how is my pretty girl? Do you want some apple to munch on," she asked, as she held out her hand to the horse. The horse wasted no time eating that piece of apple out of her hand.

After she fed Muffin, she took her out of her stall. She climbed on and began on the trail that was behind the barn. It was dusk, and a little chilly, chillier than normal for a September evening. The sky was amazing, shades of pink, orange and yellow, as it set into the trees.

Riding always helped her to focus and destress. Muffin was her therapy.

She finished riding the trail, and walked Muffin back into her stall. Then she picked up a brush and started combing her hair and mane. Chrissy began talking to the horse as if she were her therapist, as if she would really be able to give her advice. It was the simple fact that she could just let go and spill her guts. She knew that the horse wasn't going to offer her advice, or judge her. She would just stand there and listen, if she was even paying attention to what she was saying.

"Well Muffin, I'm not sure what to do anymore. There are certain clients that I can never please. I wish I could tell this woman exactly what I thought and where I'd like her to go, but she and her husband are pretty influential in this town. I can't afford to lose her as a client."

The horse snorted, as if she agreed with her. It was that kind of response that kept Chrissy sane. It was the listening ear of a mere horse that calmed her nerves and allowed her to go home to her family with a better attitude. She refuses to take her frustrations out on them.

Her ride home was much easier tonight.

Chapter 4

Eva opens the salon at 9am every day, like clockwork. She turns the dark corridor into a brightly lit space where transformation takes place on a daily basis.

As she walks to the back room to start the coffee, hot water for hot tea, and checks on the laundry bins, she breathes in deep and revels in the quiet peaceful silence while she can. Soon it will be a consistent stream of noise.

Eva grabbed a load of towels and threw them into the washer, checked the garbage cans, collected all the full baskets from the night before, put them into a larger garbage bag. Then headed out the back door to the alley where the salon's trash bin is located.

The alley is narrow and dark with red brick buildings on both sides. In the very back there is a rusted metal fire escape, beneath that, a big garbage bin sits. Today there's a strange stench coming from the end, where she was heading.

Eva walked back towards the trash bin, where on the stairwell she spotted the source of the stench. She backed up quickly at the sight in front of her tripped, and let out a scream for help. She was scooting herself back on her butt with her feet and hands moving as quickly as they'd go.

"Somebody, anybody, HELP!!"

The body was dangling lifelessly off the stairs. The face, too bloody to tell who it was. The hair was completely missing. The skull in some places, exposed. You could hear the drops of blood hitting the already large puddle of red on the cement alley.

Eva got to her feet and ran back inside. She grabbed her phone and called 911.

"911, what is your emergency," the operator asked.

"I'm at A Cut Above Salon and Spa downtown. There is a body in our alley. You have to send someone quick," Eva yelled into the phone.

"Ma'am, are you injured?"

"No, just get someone here now."

"I've already dispatched the necessary emergency crews. Did you see what happened?"

"No, I didn't. I came into work and was taking out the garbage, and found them on the stairwell."

"Was the victim conscious at all, or able to say anything, before you called us?"

"No. Nothing. Why?"

"In case they may have said how it happened or who had done this to them. I can record it for the police report."

"Oh, I see. I hate to say it, but this person did not last long after what happened to them. I've never seen anything like this. I hear the sirens now. Thank you. Are we finished here? I need to let them in the front entrance."

"Yes ma'am, we're done."

Eva hung up with the overly calm, annoyingly cool dispatcher, to run to the front door to flag down the emergency vehicles that she could see arriving.

Once the EMTs exited their vehicle, there were police cars arriving on the scene. There had to have been at least three police cars, an ambulance, the coroner's van, and the crime scene team van, all behind them.

Eva took them all through the salon and out the back to the alley.

After surveying the scene, pronouncing the victim indeed deceased, and the crime scene tape went up around the perimeter, the CSIs went to work. The police officers were talking among themselves, but Eva overheard part of their conversation.

"You know who that is right," asked the one officer, to the others.

"Is it really her," said another.

"How can you tell," asked the other one.

"Isn't that the necklace Baylor bought her, that cost close to a cool million? It was the talk of the town when she sported that sucker at the Art Gala last year."

Eva choked when she heard the name Baylor, as in Trudy Baylor. In her head, Eva kept denying that it could be her. She was just in the day before getting her hair done. Her eyes were as big as saucers when it hit her, that it could actually be Trudy Baylor, dead, in the back of the salon.

One of the plainclothes officers or investigators, she guessed, was walking toward her, notebook and pencil in hand.

"Ms. St. Claire is it? May I ask you a few questions, I'm Lieutenant Murphy ".

"Of course, anything."

"We believe the victim is Mrs. Trudy Baylor. Do you know her?"

Yes, she's a frequent client of the salon. One of our owners does her hair."

"And, who is that?" he asked, with more interest than she liked.

"That would be Chrissy Cramer. There are four owners, but Chrissy did Trudy's hair all the time."

"Do you know why Mrs. Baylor would be here? Did she have an appointment last night?"

"I'm not sure why she would have been here. She had a hair appointment yesterday morning, but that's the only one I was aware of."

"I'm sorry Ms. St. Claire, I only have a few more questions. I know this can't be very easy for you. It's not every day that you come to work and end up finding a dead body. You wouldn't happen to know of anyone here who might have had a reason to harm Mrs. Baylor, do you?"

"No one I can think of. The only contact I have ever had with her, has been when she is here getting her hair done."

In Eva's head, she was visioning the incident from yesterday, when Trudy had her little hissy and Chrissy made her feel two inches tall. She really hoped that no one here had anything to do with this horrible act.

Startled out of her thoughts, Lieutenant Murphy asked, "who is the one who does her hair again?"

"That would be one of the owners, Chrissy Cramer. Speaking of which, I should really get a hold of all the owners to let them know of the situation and get them down here. They should really be here."

"That's a good idea, I'd like to be able to ask them all some questions. Could you please have them come as soon as they can?"

"Sure, let me just go inside and make some calls. I'll use my cell phone, in case the CSI team needs to do their thing."

He smiled at her, and said "That would be perfect. Thank you for all your help."

"My pleasure."

Eva headed inside to make the calls to the girls. Her hands were shaking as she typed the numbers into the phone. The situation hadn't quite fully hit her yet.

First person to call would be Chrissy.

After telling her the news, and her totally freaking out, she said she would be in as soon as possible.

The rest of the calls she made, went pretty much along the same way. Now all they had to do was wait until everyone got there and Lieutenant Murphy could question them.

Chapter 5

Chrissy was the first to arrive. Lt. Murphy took her to the back room to question her.

"Ms. Cramer, is it?"

"Mrs., but yes. You can call me Chrissy."

"Okay. Chrissy. I need to ask you a few questions and it shouldn't take too long. I am just trying to establish the relationship between you, this salon, and the victim.

How do you know Mrs. Baylor?"

"She was a longtime client of mine. I would do her hair once a week. I have no idea who would do such a horrific thing to her."

"And where were you last night?"

"Me? I was out at my barn with my horse, taking in a trail ride and grooming her. Why?"

"Can anyone vouch for your whereabouts? Did anyone see you?"

"I'm sorry, am I a suspect," Chrissy asked, in a bit of a panicked tone.

"You're not a suspect. We do need to establish that everyone who works here and anyone who has access to this building has an alibi. Now, did anyone see you last night?"

"I was at the barn by myself riding. I don't remember if I saw anyone out there."

"Well, you're going to have to remember. Did you have any issues with Mrs. Baylor?"

"No," Chrissy lied.

Her anxiety level and blood pressure were reaching catastrophic levels. A stroke or heart attack was going to surface, much sooner than she thought.

"Mrs. Cramer, whatever you do don't leave town," Lt. Murphy said, suspiciously.

He walked out the door and towards the front where the rest of the girls were sitting and waiting for their turn to get questioned.

Once he was finished with everyone, Emma waltzed in and stared at everyone's stoic faces.

"What's up with all the police tape and cop cars, did someone die?"

"Oh my god Emma. Did you not get my message? Yes, someone died. Someone was brutally murdered in the back alley last night. I found her body this morning while I was taking out the garbage. It was Mrs. Baylor," Eva was trying to explain.

"Whoa, you're freaking kidding me. I didn't get the message, my phone died. Sorry, bad choice of words. Hey Chrissy, did you finally take her out after yesterday?"

"Emma, shut up!"

Eva was trying hard to get Emma to zip her mouth.

"Excuse me, do you work here," Murphy questioned Emma, with a serious look.

"Yes, I'm a stylist here. Emma Walker, at your service."

"You need to come with me, Emma. We need to ask you a few questions."

Emma and Lt. Murphy headed to the back room, and Chrissy was about to throw up.

"Oh my god, oh my god... what is she trying to do to me? He already thinks I have something to do with this. I swear, I don't. I was riding Muffin on the trail and brushing her in the barn last night, then I went home. If I can't find someone to vouch for me, they're going to arrest me."

"Calm down Chrissy. I believe you, we all believe you," said Chelsea.

Chelsea, always being a calm and confident woman, was also an owner. She worked the spa side and did nails. She sat to the right of Chrissy, holding her hand in hers. She is always the epitome of style and trend. She has flowing shoulder-length brown hair, bronzed skin, and impeccable looking nails. All the girls shook their heads in agreement. They knew Chrissy wasn't capable of doing anything so heinous.

"We may need to call our lawyer, Jerry. Since this happened in the back of our business, just to let him know what happened. Not because I think you had anything to do with it Chrissy," Chelsea said.

Chelsea also sported the most smartass, sarcastic attitude of the group.

"Yes, that's probably a good idea. Call him, and tell him we may need him," Chrissy said.

"Shannon, you should call Jerry. He likes you. Sweet talk him. Tell him everything is fine. None of us are hurt and we are all innocent," Chelsea laughed.

"Why do I have to call him?"

As Chelsea was about to make her case about why Shannon was a good candidate to do the calling of the lawyer, Emma and Lt. Murphy came walking out of the back room. Emma's face was that of an apologetic friend, who may or may not have said something she shouldn't have. Murphy's was more that of an annoyed cop.

Emma mouthed the words, "I'm sorry" in Chrissy's direction.

Chrissy was surprised and wasn't sure what that meant. What could she have told him?

"Ms. Cramer, can we talk," asked Murphy.

"Sure."

She followed the Lt. to the back room, and he shut the door for privacy.

"Would you like to tell me anything about what happened yesterday between you and Trudy Baylor?"

"I wouldn't call it an anything that would result in murder. Yes, we, or I should say, she had a problem with me yesterday. I was running two minutes behind. She believes she is the Queen of Sheba, and I should drop everything I am doing, just to bow to her. I,simply, in a very nice way told her she could take her business elsewhere, if she was dissatisfied with my work. I'd hardly constitute that as motive for me to murder her."

25

"So, you never actually threatened her or her life," he asked.

"Never! I also have witnesses as to what was said. They are all there in the front, as well as some clients that happened to be in the salon. What Emma told you, was hearsay, because she wasn't even in the salon at the time this all happened."

Lt. Murphy didn't look convinced, but he now knew a little more of what happened yesterday morning, and it still didn't fully exonerate Chrissy, but he also knew how much Mrs. Baylor liked to make people feel small.

Just as he and Chrissy exited the room, the front door of the shop opened and in walked Jerry Grimes, Lawyer extraordinaire. He was a stocky man with a big nose and receding hairline. He always looked like he had just stepped out of a Mafia movie. He resembled a larger version of Joe Pesci. You know the type: black slicked back hair, pinstripe suit, black wingtip shoes, gold pinky ring, along with a very expensive looking Rolex watch.

"Ladies... what do we have going on here today," he asked.

They all looked at him as though they had just been sent to the principal's office. Not one of them wanted to make the first remark. Finally, Eva stood up and explained the whole incident, and how she was the one who found the body. The look on his face was blank, not grim, not happy, not anything. The girls sat there stock-still, waiting for something to come out of his mouth. A minute went by, which felt like hours, and he finally moved to the lieutenant and asked to speak to him in private. They both shuffled their way to the same back room where he had taken the girls to speak with in private.

"Mr. Grimes, is it? I know you are the owner's lawyer, and I am not about to sugarcoat the severity of this homicide to you. I will get right to the point. Mrs. Cramer has motive and no one to vouch for her whereabouts last night. She says she was at her horse barn, taking care of her horse. Until someone can verify that, she is our main suspect."

"Okay tell me, what is her motive? Losing one client would be no big deal for these girls, they are booked more than 99% of the time. They don't even need to advertise their shop. That's how good the business is."

The lieutenant stood listening to the salon's lawyer drone on and on while chewing on his cheek deep in thought. The number one suspect doesn't have an alibi. He wasn't going to downplay it to any of them. He knew each of them could have a motive. He would weed out the innocent soon enough. Right now, it looks bad for all the stylists and the salon.

The look on Chrissy's face when the men exited the back room was a mix of pure horror and a scared to death little girl. She just looked into her hands, as if they held the answers.

They all sat there in silence while the police and investigators were cleaning up and starting to head out.

Soon clients would start to trickle in, and they would get wind of what had happened.

Eva was already calling clients to cancel appointments for the day until they got the okay to go ahead.

Chapter 6

It was about noon when everything was cleaned up. The officers and investigators were cleared of the area, and everything looked somewhat normal again.

The girls, still sitting in stunned wonder, didn't quite know what to do or say to each other. Eva looked around and knew something had to be done. She hated seeing her friends and co-workers so down and out.

"Hey, you all know this is crap. Chrissy could never have done this. I, for one, believe her. We all should. I don't think anyone in this room did it and we need to act as if everything is normal, or at least try to. I've called all your clients and told them we had to close for the day, but we will get them rescheduled ASAP."

They looked up at her with small smiles on their faces. They couldn't deny she was right and they had to put on their professional faces and get through this day, no matter what.

Emma stood and declared, "Eva's right, we can't let this get to us. There are people, most notably, down the street, who would love to see us all go down. We just have to let this play out. I know they will find out who offed Mrs. Baylor. I'm sorry Chrissy that I opened my big mouth. I never meant to get you in trouble."

Chrissy gave Emma a sincere smile, but you could tell she was worried. She knew she wasn't the one who killed her, she couldn't think of anyone she knew, who had such an evil mentality level. All she kept thinking about was how horrible and painful it must have been for Trudy to die that way. It was beyond gruesome. It was definitely the work of someone who was psychotic.

While still in her own head, Chrissy didn't even seem to notice the bustling of movement around her. All the girls were staring at her.

"Why are all of you looking at me," she asked, annoyed. She got up and walked through the group, to get a cup of coffee, her head hanging low, distraught and a little lightheaded.

Eva walked over to Chrissy and sat down next to her. She placed her hand on her shoulder and looked in her eyes, and said "I know in my heart, you had nothing to do with this. Somehow, we will prove it." They looked at each other and smiled.

Chrissy thanked God that someone truly believed her. "I'm not going to let this get me! I've got too much to do and too many people counting on me."

With that, she walked over to her station and busied herself. She was trying to make it look like she was trying to organize her station, but they all knew Chrissy was doing her best not to lose her shit.

As the day went by, Eva looked at all of the girls, they meant the world to her. She knew without reservation, that not one of them was capable of doing this.

The salon was so quiet except for the occasional ringing of the phone, it was all but eerie. Most of the girls had headed home for the day, but not before checking on Eva. They thought she may have been traumatized after what she had seen that morning.

Little did they know Eva has seen her fair share of traumatic events in her life. Eva was bound to never let anyone find out about her secret she couldn't let anyone know. It was imperative that it stayed over twenty years in the past.

The looks the girls were giving her were starting to annoy her. Yes she found a disgusting blood corpse this morning. Yes it was horrible and scary. She just wanted them to give it a rest and not have to visualize it anymore.

Eva was just feeling annoyed. She was thinking about something while visualizing the whole scene over again, giving way for an idea. Not an idea she was too keen to have thought, but it just may be what saves her friend and boss's life.

She spent the rest of the day trying to think of other ways of helping, but nothing as good as her first one seemed to make sense. She'd have to do a little more research and put a little more thought into whether it was worth trying.

The rest of the day, she was hopeful, but also nervous. Her husband would not be happy with this crazy idea of hers, but she was thinking of the bigger picture.

She could potentially exonerate her friend. Wasn't that for the greater good?

How the thoughts in her head were jumbled with pros and cons of this ridiculous scheme she was trying to form. As if he could read her thoughts, the phone rang and Kris was on the other end; he had just seen the news of what had happened earlier.

"Eva, are you okay," he asked.

No hello, just straight to fear and worry in his voice. Eva smiled, she could hear his worry and she appreciated his protective side and loved him for it.

"I'm fine. It was Mrs. Baylor. Did you know her?"

"Oh wow! That old lady you were talking about last night?"

"Yes the same one."

She went on and told him the whole story from beginning to end, and he just let her tell it.

"Holy shit Eva! How's Chrissy doing?"

"She's hanging in there. Kris, I know she didn't have anything to do with this, I don't think any of the girls did; it had to be someone outside this shop, I can feel it."

"Oh no! No, no, no..."

He knew exactly what she was thinking, and he didn't like it, one bit. "Eva, you promised."

Eva cut him off.

"We'll talk about it later. I have to go. I love you," and she hung up.

"Everything okay, Eva," Shannon asked, clearly overhearing her conversation with her husband.

"Yeah everything is fine, Kris just gets a little over-protective and worries too much. I assured him I was fine."

"Honey, if you're not okay, we would totally understand if you need a couple of days off. I don't know what I would have done in your situation. I probably would have passed out, woke up and screamed, and passed out again. You kept your wits about you and called 911."

"Yeah, I'm still not sure how that happened," she laughed. "But really, I am okay. I don't need any time off, but thank you for the offer and the concern."

"Well if you change your mind, just let us know," as she walked away.

Eva was thoughtful for a minute, and now was sure that these girls couldn't have had anything to do with this. It was absurd.

Looking at the time it was already almost 5pm. The day was coming to a close, even though the salon was closed all day. Eva kept busy making calls, rescheduling clients, and making sure all the towels and capes were washed, dried, folded, and put away. It kept her busy for the most part. She finished payroll and paying the bills like normal. That made her feel like it was a normal day. Though Eva admitted... "this is anything but normal."

Chapter 7

Chrissy was quiet but internally she was screaming. She was genuinely worried about her future and her family. In her head, she couldn't help but wonder if Lieutenant Murphy really did think she was the killer. Would he do anymore investigating into any of Trudy's other acquaintances? She couldn't help but think that she wasn't the only one Trudy pissed off on a weekly basis.

Her thoughts drifted to the three girls they couldn't get a hold of earlier. Sarah was taking care of her sick mother. Georgia was still just getting back from the Bahamas. Charlene? She didn't know why she hadn't responded to the texts or calls. She thought that was a little strange but she'd worry about that later. Right now, she wanted this day to be over and go home to her family. Her husband, Jason, had called earlier to check on her, and her daughters had come in to give her hugs and love, which is probably what had gotten her through this day. She was mentally done and there was a glass of wine, or possibly two or three with her name on them.

Looking around at her shop, that she was part owner of, she was so proud of what they had accomplished in such a short time. They were booked 90% of the time, and people raved about them on social media. Everyday they were getting calls from potential new clients. It was a far cry from where they worked before that was for sure. The owners of the salon they all had come from, were horrible people to work for. They were paid only in commission, which robbed them of money. The girls vowed when they opened their shop it would be chair rent based. Basically their renters would be able to be their own bosses. They would keep all the money they made, except for a weekly rent that they paid, and they could make their own hours. Thankfully, it has worked out very well, so far.

While in her deep internal thought, she was startled when Emma had come over and gave her a quick hug.

"Emma... why are you hugging me," she asked.

"Sorry, I feel guilty for putting all those thoughts into Lt. Murphy's head. It's probably the only reason he's locked onto you as a main suspect."

"I'm sure they would have found out about our disagreement some other way, even if you hadn't said anything," Chrissy said, trying to make her feel less guilty.

She waved goodnight to Emma and finished cleaning up her station, so she could take off. She was about to leave when her phone started ringing. Her cell phone, not the salon phone. She didn't recognize the number; so she let it go to voicemail. As she left, she made sure every door and gate were securely locked.

Seeing the yellow and black police tape made her sigh. She climbed into her car and sat there for a second, thinking and lamenting on her present situation.

"How did I get to this point? What did I do to deserve this," she cried and punched the steering wheel.

Looking at her phone she noticed a voicemail was waiting. She didn't remember her phone ringing recently. Then it hit her, the number she hadn't recognized. Now there was a message.

Pressing the voicemail button hesitantly she waited for the message to start. Nothing could have prepared her for this.

"Hello Chrissy," said a voice that didn't even sound human. "Sorry to hear about the incident earlier at your shop. In all honesty Mrs. Baylor deserved everything she got. It was however, way too easy to get her to meet me there. I couldn't believe she actually showed up. Don't you think it was quite symbolic that her head full of that beautiful hair that you had undoubtedly recently done was completely scalped? Her screams were delicious and reminiscent of the horror movies I love so much. It brought me such great pleasure to inflict all of this pain on her and you. The best part is, I hear you are the cops number one suspect," it said, laughing. "Oh, that was just priceless. Watch your back. I'm not done yet. You will go down." Click

Chrissy's hands were shaking and tears were running down her face. She was scared. She knew the only thing she could do was to go to the police and let them hear the message. This demented message would surely put her in the clear. They could trace the phone number and find out who it was. As for the voice on the other end, she had no clue who it could be. It was so distorted, they must have used a voice scrambler.

She pulled into the Delaware Police Department parking lot, jumped out of her car and ran for the door. Fumbling her way through security, she finally got to the front desk and asked for Lt. Murphy. The lady behind the desk was old. She had been there all day and was not in the mood for more work.

"What is it you need dear," she asked.

"I need to see Lieutenant Murphy, like now!"

"What in God's name is this regarding?"

"Just tell him Chrissy Cramer is here," she said, in a panicked tone.

The old lady at the desk shot straight up out of her seat like she'd seen a ghost. "Oh my God! You're the one they believe killed Trudy Baylor. You stay right there." She yelled to the officer by the security screen, "Hey George, this is Chrissy Cramer. Get over here and watch that she doesn't leave, while I go get Lt. Murphy."

The security guard ran over to her and held her arm tightly. Chrissy gave a little wince.

"Easy there gumshoe I'd like my arm to remain in its socket." He merely grumbled at her.

Within minutes Lt. Murphy was at the front desk, walking Chrissy to his office. She looked around and noticed everyone was staring at her. They all knew who she was now. It wasn't for her amazing hairstyles or fabulous hair colors that she was famous for either. It was

37

because she was now the suspected killer of high society matriarch Trudy Baylor.

"What can I help you with, Mrs. Cramer?"

"For one, you can tell these people staring at me, that I am innocent until proven guilty," she said, grimacing.

"I'm sorry they're all staring, news and gossip travels fast around here apparently," he apologized.

"But seriously, what can I help you with?"

Chrissy had all but forgotten why she was there in the first place.

"This! Listen to this voicemail I just received. Unfortunately, I can't decipher whose voice it is, but maybe you can."

She pressed the play button and let him hear for himself. He had a disgusted look on his face and when it finished. he said,

"You don't know who sent this?"

"No, I got a call from a number I didn't recognize. I didn't pick it up and the message was left."

"Do you still have the number in your phone?"

She pulled the number from her previous calls and gave it to him in the hopes that he could possibly trace it.

He took the phone and left the office. She guessed he was taking it to some forensics
team, for all she knew.

The Lieutenant returned not looking too positive, and that made her more nervous.

"So, were you able to trace it, or get the owner's name," she asked, hopeful.

"No, it was a burner phone and you can't trace those. Also the voice is completely distorted. For all we know it could be anyone, male or female. You could have had a friend or family member send that in hopes of taking the focus off of you. Is that what you did," he asked, accusingly.

"Not at all! I would never even think of doing that. I don't have that kind of evil imagination, thank you very much."

She got up then and turned on her heel and headed for the exit.

Chrissy was now at her wits end. Everything was still pointing to her and wondering how to make them believe her. She sat in her car for a few minutes, pondering her life, and how quickly things had taken such an awful turn. She just wanted to get home and be with her family now.

Her drive was quiet, but short. Delaware, Ohio isn't a metropolis by any means. Everything was very close, even her house. Her house was brightly lit as it was already dark already, but she felt safe and couldn't wait to get inside.

Chapter 8

Eva reached her street, and was dreading the conversation she knew she was going to have with Kris. She knew this might be the only way to get her friend and boss off the hook for murder.

Pulling into her driveway, she stared at her beautiful home thinking of all the wonderful memories that she, Kris and her kids have made there. It was a far cry from her childhood, that was for sure.

Her mind started to wander to that day. The day she gave up everything she'd ever known so she could have a normal life. A life her parents never gave her.

Eva didn't have a normal upbringing. Her past is a troubled one and one that she wishes to keep there.

Her parents, along with her and her sister were witches. Not the witches you read about in children's books, but real spell casting witches.

For the most part, her grandmother was an earth witch, she believed in thanking the air, the water, fire and the ground for everything.

Then there was her mother; she would conjure up spells for everything under the sun. She would do spells for love, money, illness, revenge, you name it. She charged people exorbitant amounts of money for her to perform rituals.

Neither parent worked your normal 9-5 job. Her mother had made money by being a sideshow freak. Her father, much like her grandmother, did more farming, planted herbs and vegetables and sold them at the local markets. Her father would use spells to improve his crops.

Eva hated the magic her mother did, and even refused to participate. Her mother would punish her, every time she refused to participate.

That night in December, 1989, was the day that changed everything. It was the Winter Solstice, and as always, it was the time of the "Return of Light" celebration to begin.

In Eva's case, however, her mother and other witches celebrate the "Magic of the Darkness". Her mom believed in the darker side of magic, because it kept her enemies at bay. On this particular night, in the deep woods of Connecticut, a fire burned bright, and the family gathered around, telling stories of the Gods and their reckoning with the Underworld or Netherworld as some perceived it. It is said that Inanna, the Goddess of Light cannot shine until she meets her sister in the Underworld.

On that night, her family met with darkness and evil. Eva's mother Alma started the Winter Solstice ritual, as she always had, but threw a spell into the flames along, which Eva had never before seen or heard of. The flames began to swirl and dance, the wind picked up as the leaves on the ground spun around them.

A silhouette started to form in the flames. First the horns, then a larger head, followed by a skinnier torso. It seemed half human, half animal, but it was hard for her to tell what emerged from the flames. Eva's eyes grew as big and round as saucers.   She was fixated on the large figure. Her sister Ameilia began screaming, while her father was swearing at their mother in at least five languages. Alma smiled, her eyes closed, and her arms lifted to the sky, as if she were praising God himself. She ignored her surrounding family's cries and screams.

  Sebastian, Eva's father, began trying a new spell, to rid the fire of the creature that was emerging. Her mother quickly put a stop to it and in turn put a spell on him.   He was shut down.

  The girls looked on in horror. Their father was paralyzed in his spot. Their mother was gaining more momentum and power as she was welcoming the beast to take full form.

  Eva, the oldest of the two girls, was trying to gain some composure. She needed to think properly, but it was difficult while taking in the scene around her. She had fully believed that her mother had lost her mind.

  Eva ran over to where her mother was standing, grabbed her and shook her hard.

  "Stop this Mom! You can't do this!" she yelled.

  Alma looked her daughter in the eyes, but this wasn't her mother looking back at her. This was not the mother she knew and loved. Her eyes were onyx black, and not the beautiful hazel that she had inherited from her.

  The creature was no longer dancing in the flames, it was nowhere to be seen; or so she thought.

She looked at her mother again, closer and longer. Reality kicked in, and hit her like a brick. This was not her mother, at least not now. The evil entity had inhabited her mother's body now.

"What have you done with my mother," she screamed in her face.

A deep menacing voice permeated throughout the woods, coming out of her mouth. The creature inside her mother replied, "Your mother is dead."

"I don't believe you. She's still in there. You're holding her hostage in her own body, you son of a bitch!"

Eva pushed the creature, hoping to knock it over, but it didn't budge. It appeared to be getting angrier.

It whipped its arms out, and with all its energy, made Eva fly through the air, and land thirty feet from the fire into a large tree trunk. She landed hard, hitting her head.

Amelia ran to check on her, crying and terrified.

"Eva! Are you okay?

Eva's head was going to hurt like hell in the morning, but she had to push that aside for now. She got up feeling a little dizzy, and for a second she couldn't get everything to stop spinning. Once the movement stopped enough for her to move her feet forward, she went to her father's side to check on him.

"Daddy, are you able to move? I need your help. Can you talk?"

She pleaded with her father, desperate for him to show any signs of life or movement.

His eyes were the only thing that could speak to her. They were sad and apologetic. Eva's shoulders slumped in defeat, as she looked down at her father. The tears rolling down her cheeks, she cried.

"Why did you bring children into this family? Witchcraft has brought nothing but pain to us. I hate it! It's not right. It's evil, and I hate you both for doing this to us!"

A single tear fell from her father's eyes. She knew if they were going to survive this night, she was going to have to be the one to do it.

Looking in the direction of the creature that was once her mother, she was slack jawed at the site of it dancing around the bonfire. It was chanting in some strange native tongue. Eva turned to ignore the display of evil.

She couldn't bear to think of what she was going to have to do. Right now it was the only thing she could think to do, or they would never survive this horrible night.

Eva gathered all her strength, all her power and pulled all of her sister's and father's internal magic from them, too. It was easy, they were in so much shock that their defenses were low.

She walked slowly, quietly and determined toward the evil. Her head high, her shoulders back, all while carefully making her way towards her mother. She stopped within three feet of her mother. With one strong push of her arms stretched out in front of her, and with a loud scream, she used every bit of magic and energy she could muster. A white light emerged from her fingertips and her mother went straight into the fire, head first.

The flames screamed with anger, turned blue, then red and back to orange. You could see two separate beings flailing about in the fire. They were separating from each other and dying together.

Eva collapsed to the cold ground, her head in her hands, crying uncontrollably and her body was shaking. A hand touched the back of her head, stroking it lightly. The touch scared her, and she swung her head up to see her father standing there. The spell Alma had put on him had broken the moment she died. He was now trying to comfort his daughter.

"Daddy, are you okay," she asked.

"I'm okay, just a little woozy. Are you okay my dear," he asked gently.

"I've killed her. I killed mom," she declared.

"I know sweetheart, I saw everything. I am so sorry, Eva. I'm sorry it had to be you, to do it. You shouldn't blame yourself dear, it was purely self-defense and you saved us. It should have been me, who saved our family, not you."

They sat there on the ground, embracing each other, grieving their loss. After that night, Eva vowed to leave Connecticut and never to practice witchcraft again, until now.

A knock on her car window scared her out of her trip down memory lane. It was her daughter, Alma.

"Mom, are you coming in, you've been out here for twenty minutes."

"Alma, you frightened me. I must have been daydreaming. I'm coming in now," she said, as she stepped out of her car.

Eva had to shake the memories she had just brought forth. She hadn't thought of that night in a long time.

Chapter 9

Walking into the house, Eva saw Kris standing there with his arms open. He took his wife into his arms and gave her a hug and a kiss. She looked forward to this every evening, though his hug was a little tighter and lasted a little longer than usual, Eva didn't seem to mind. Tonight she needed it. This had been a bad day.

"How are you doing," he asked, already knowing the answer.

"I've been better. We need to talk, but, I need you to just listen, without judgement."

"Eva, I already have an idea about what you want to talk about and I don't like it. You told me if you ever decided to do any type of spell, to stop you. I am taking that statement seriously, and I am asking you not to do it."

"I know what I said, and I have never done or wanted to do any type of witchcraft, since that night. I don't see any other way around it. I told you, you needed to listen to what I had to say, and I meant it. Please Kris, I am begging you, just listen," she pleaded.

"Fine I'll listen," he stated, as he followed her.

They headed off to their den, where they could have some sort of privacy, away from the kids. The den was their quiet place for solitude and relaxing, without a lot of noise. It looked like the inside of a psychologist's office with the ornate cherry wooden desk and matching chair and comfy chocolate brown leather couch. The matching cherry bookshelves covered a whole wall. It was painted light gray, with white chair rail. They hadn't put a TV in this room. They did that on purpose. This was the room Kris and Eva went to, to have their talks, whether it was about the kids, money, vacation planning or just to get some quiet time together. This is where they would retreat to, and the kids knew not to bother their parents, if they were in there.

Eva sat on the couch looking beat, but ready for a serious and convincing argument ahead of her. Kris sat at the other end of the couch, with his knee sideways, so he could face her. He was ready to hear her out.

"Okay, before you say no, I implore you to listen to everything I have to say. I want you to think it through before you make any kind of snide remark. Can you agree to do that," she asked, truly determined to win the argument.

"I promise, now let's just get on with it please."

"You know I have not done any type of witchcraft since 1989, and I swore I would never do it again. There comes a time, where it could come in handy, in a good way, not used for bad."

Kris' face curled up into a scowl, but he relaxed and let her proceed without a word.

"I know for a fact that there is a spell I can cast that will let me see exactly what happened last night in the alley. It has never had any bad repercussions, and I will take every precaution. I will even let you come with me and watch me perform it, if it makes you feel better."

She was cursing herself for saying that, because she didn't want him to see her this way.

She looked at her husband, waiting for some reaction, but there was none, so she continued.

"This spell will actually be like watching a video, it shows the people, place and everything that happened. If I can do this; if you let me perform this one spell, it could potentially save Chrissy from life in jail, or worse. I have to try, Kris."

He knew whatever he was thinking was not what Eva was going to want to hear, so he put on his understanding husband's face, and took her hand.

"I don't like this idea at all. I think it is dangerous messing with magic and spells. You of all people know what can happen. What if it goes wrong? I understand your dilemma and wanting to help your friend. I'm just worried, but I will support you in this one spell. Please do not ask me to do this again."

Eva threw her arms around her husband and hugged him tight. She thanked him over and over again, for his support.

She asked him if he was going to go with her and watch, but he reluctantly declined. He knew in his heart, he could not watch his wife practice witchcraft.

Even though she was relieved, she also felt a little upset. She could hardly be mad at him though.

After dinner was over and cleaned up, Eva retreated back to the den and began her research on spells that would conjure up past events.

She stopped for a moment and looked up to the ceiling, praying to God that this would work. She desperately wanted to help her friend. Closing her eyes for a moment as she said a silent prayer, she shook herself and continued her search.

There were so many more spells than she realized for this type of thing. How would she know which one was the best for this situation?

Then she saw one that stood out from the rest...

"This one, this is it!" she yelled.

All of a sudden she felt more excited. She figured she could gather all of the supplies she needed and do it tomorrow night after dark, when no one would be around.

Feeling a little more positive about things, Eva fell into an exhaustion induced sleep and stayed asleep.

Chapter 10

Emma had arrived home, after what could only be described as the worst day of her life. She couldn't believe that she could be responsible for sending her friend, and boss to jail for murder. She had no idea that her statement could be made into a huge deal.

Grabbing a bottle of wine from the fridge and pouring herself a large glass, Emma was quite thankful that her kids were with her ex-husband tonight.

Sitting on her couch, she turned the TV on and of course the news was on. A picture of Trudy Baylor, Delaware's elite socialite took up over a quarter of the screen. Emma wanted to puke, and not from the wine.

"People are probably glad she's dead," she said to the TV. "She was a grade A bitch and everyone thought that, they just didn't vocally project their thoughts, or she would make life unlivable."

Emma of all people should know. Trudy Baylor ruined her life. As if remembering the memory from four years ago, Emma winced. She thought about the day that her world was turned upside down.

Emma continued sipping her wine, while the memories resurfaced of what Trudy had done to her and her family.

Her kids were to never know what happened, or they would hate their Dad for good. She couldn't handle that. The memories were painful to think about, but here they were, back in the forefront of her mind.

She'd been divorced now for almost three and half years, and it was Trudy Baylor's fault.

Emma and Jack Walker were pretty happy. They had been high school sweethearts and best friends most of their lives.

Jack and his work buddies had always taken a yearly trip to Las Vegas. A guy's week. It never bothered Emma that he'd go off on his man-cation. She herself would go on spa weekends with her girlfriends, now and then. She never felt her relationship or marriage to Jack was in Jeopardy, and she trusted him to nth degree.

They had four daughters, and he had always been a hands-on Dad and husband. They were the A-typical postcard family, with their moderately large house, white picket fence and the big dog running a muck in the yard. Everyone's dream life... until Jack's man-cation that summer four years ago.

You know that saying, "What happens in Vegas, stays in Vegas?" Well unfortunately what happened in Vegas, came back with Jack, in a box with a red ribbon attached.

Jack had returned from Vegas. He relayed the calamity of crazy stories and $200 poorer. Everything had been normal.

Two days after he had returned, Emma received an envelope addressed to her only, with no return address. It was wrapped with a red satin ribbon.

Curiosity got to her, so she opened it immediately. Inside were photos, a thumb drive and a handwritten letter from Trudy Baylor.

She couldn't even comprehend what she was looking at. Photos of her husband making out with another man, a man she didn't even recognize. They were definitely taken in Vegas, she couldn't mistake the background.

She held up the thumb drive and said, "What the hell could be on this?"

Emma wasn't sure she could handle any more surprises, and wasn't sure she wanted to know what was on it.

Holding up the letter, she started reading it, and as anything from Trudy Baylor, it started off smugly.

Emma dear,

We were recently in Las Vegas, for business and couldn't help but spot Jack and his work buddies while we were there. Happy accident. But, after what we had seen, we thought it only appropriate that we inform you of your husbands' extra-curricular activities while away.

Apparently, you're not doing your job as wife and lover.

Just thought you'd want to know.

Sincerely,
Trudy

"Are you freaking kidding me," she yelled. "Bitch!"

Jack was still at work and the kids were still in school, so she sat at her laptop. She held up the thumb drive, trying to decide whether she wanted to see anymore. She thought it couldn't be any worse than the pictures, so she inserted the drive and let it start.

Nothing could have prepared her for what she was looking at now. Not only were there more photos, but also videos.

She slammed the lid of her laptop, screaming and crying.

"I will kill them both!"

Meaning of course, Jack and Trudy.

When Jack came home from work, she had already sent the kids over to her parents, who thankfully only live one street over. She hadn't said a word to her mother about the package she received, nor had she told the kids. Emma didn't want anyone to know.

She needed to speak to Jack in private, in case she ended up killing him for real.

She was sitting at the kitchen table with her cup of coffee between her hands, when Jack walked in.

"Hey babe, where are the kids?"

"I sent them to my Mom and Dad's for a while."

As she looked up at him, he could see her eyes were red and puffy. Concern etched in his face, he knelt down in front of her.

"What's wrong Emma, you've been crying."

He was always Captain Obvious.

"Sit down Jack."

After he was seated, she pulled the envelope from her lap and slid it over to him. The blank look on his face said he had no clue what was going on.

"Open it Jack, and look at what's inside."

He opened the envelope and took out its content. Realization hit. His secret was no longer a secret. His heart began pounding in his head. He looked at Emma, but couldn't speak. The hurt in her eyes told him everything. She was never going to forgive him, or understand.

Emma started in on him. "What do you have to say Jack? Are you gay? Are bi-sexual? Do you love him? What the hell, say something," she yelled.

Jack was bombarded with question after question by Emma, and his brain was floating. He thought just then, he may have had a minor stroke.

After finding some semblance of voice control, he stuttered... "I don't know what to say Emma, other than, I'm sorry. I never meant to hurt you or the kids."

"So, you're not saying this wasn't just a one- time thing," she said. She waited for him to elaborate.

"No, it wasn't."

His head dropped in shame.

"This was never supposed to come to light. Do the kids know? Did you tell your parents?"

"Heavens No!"

That made him breathe a little easier; not much, but a little.

Their phones started going off, and text messages started pouring in. Friends and family were asking if it was true. Messages from neighbors were coming in, meaning it was going around the neighborhood, already. Everyone would know that Jack cheated, with a man.

Emma was furious. She didn't know how it could have gotten around so fast, until she remembered who had sent her the package in the first place. The package that had ruined her life.

Days went by, and Emma was afraid to leave the house. She knew people were staring at her, in pity, and not because of newly colored pink hair.

Text messages went unanswered for weeks. Her friends and family would try to call, but she'd let them all go to her voicemail. She didn't want to deal with the fact that her life, as she knew it, was over. She had kicked Jack out that first night, and subsequently filed for divorce.

The kids were so upset, and wanted answers. She couldn't tell them the truth, it would destroy them. She played it off like Mommy and Daddy weren't getting along anymore. She made sure the kids understood that it had nothing to do with them.

Emma's hatred for Trudy Baylor ran deep. She wanted to kill her. As Emma sat with her wine in hand, reliving that horrible moment, she smiled. It was just a little grin, at the knowledge that she was dead.

The smile didn't last long.

Paranoia creeped in as she thought, "they might think I had a motive to kill her. I do have every reason to want her dead. In the heat of the moment I even expressed wanting to kill her myself, but I didn't."

She sat there for a minute, in quiet thought. She then realized she had a solid alibi for last night. She had been sitting at the kitchen table with her oldest daughter, helping her with geometry.

Sinking deeper into the couch, she sighed with relief. The worry was still there for her boss though.

"Could Chrissy really be capable of doing this?"

Chapter 11

The next day, the salon was busy as usual. The vibe was significantly different. Calls were coming in, some for appointments and some were cancelling their appointments, with Chrissy.

Eva knew the sooner she'd be able to perform the spell, the better off the situation would be; not only for Chrissy, but for the salon as a whole. Business was going to start hurting, if this continued.

The day progressed and more and more no-shows were happening. It was taking its toll on Chriss.

She came to the front desk and asked Eva what the rest of her day looked like. Eva glanced at the computer screen that held all the appointments, and it showed that one of her regulars was supposed to be there fifteen minutes prior. "Another no-show," she thought.

Eva looked up at Chrissy with hope and asked, "Did you try calling Tracy, maybe she got stuck in traffic?"

"I left her a message, since she hadn't picked up the call.

"This whole mess is going to ruin my business and everything I have worked so hard to achieve. I'm going to have to file for bankruptcy."

Her eyes were glassy, as she tried to hold back the tears.

It broke Eva's heart. "I'm sure it's just the initial shock of what happened. Everything will be back to normal in a few days," she tried to sound convincing.

"I hope you're right. I'm going to go grab a sandwich, but I'll have my phone on me if you need me."

And off she went, with her head hanging low as she walked out the door.

Shannon ran up to the desk, as soon as she saw Chrissy leave, "Where is Chrissy going?"

"She just went out to grab some food."

"Oh, okay. I'm really worried about her. I know she couldn't have had anything to do with Trudy's murder, I just know it."

Eva looked up at Shannon and smiled, "I know she didn't either, and I'm sure there will be some way to prove it, too."

"God, I hope you're right."

She walked back to her station and continued on weaving color into her clients hair.

Eva was getting anxious, hopeful even, about her ability to prove Chrissy's innocence. She knew everyone would be gone by 8pm tonight. She leaves at 7pm, but she still had to pick up some supplies that she needed. There were a few things she didn't have at home.

The day seemed to drag on, and slowed way down from the normal. It was not a typical day at A Cut Above hair salon. Thankfully some of Chrissy's clients still showed up, which seemed to cheer her up some.

Darkness was fast approaching, and Eva was vibrating with anticipation at the thought of performing her upcoming experiment, as she would prefer to call it.

She hadn't practiced witchcraft in years, not even a good luck spell for her kids when they had big tests.

She meant what she said that night in the woods. She would never practice again, and she had held true to her word, until now.

The salon was starting to clear out more and more as the evening was approaching. Chrissy had left an hour prior, Shannon was just finishing and Emma was putting the finishing touches on a snotty teenage girls' hair that had to be bright blue.

Eva was packing her desk up, and getting ready to take off.

She had her list in her hand, with the list of items she needed to perform the spell.

As she headed for the gate that left out of the alley, she waved goodnight to the girls and was on her way.

They didn't know she was coming back, and they didn't need to know.

Chapter 12

First stop on Eva's list was the Dollar Store. It was one place she could get cheap white pillar candles. She didn't typically have the wider white candles around her house. She was more of a Bath and Body Works, stinky three wick candle girl.

Luckily, this was an easy find. She had the salt, powder and a jar of pig's blood in the bag that she threw in the car this morning.

The pigs blood had been stowed away in her wooden chest that she had hidden in the basement for the last 20 years. She had had no need for it, and it's not something she would keep out in the open.

Now she only needed to find a white silk scarf. She thought this item may be a little harder to find quickly. She gave herself two places that were close, and had the best possibility of having one, which was Meijer and Kohls. Both places pretty much had everything you could want.

First stop was Meijer. They weren't as expensive. She figured she would only use it this one time, so nothing too elaborate was needed.

Strike one, Meijer did not have a white silk scarf. They had every other color under the rainbow, but no white. She headed to Kohl's. They had cotton, flannel and wool, but she couldn't find silk.

"Why is it so hard to find a white silk scarf," she said to herself.

This was the one item she most certainly had to get. This wasn't one she could pass on,and use something else in its place. The white silk scarf was for her safety, otherwise she would forget all about trying to do this spell.

She saw a floor person near purses, so she walked quickly in her direction. In a polite, but rushed tone she asked the young girl if they had any white silk scarves, and if they did, where they would be.

Tonight was her lucky night. The girl walked her over to the accessories' area, where they had dressier earrings, bracelets and scarves. They had silk scarves in a multitude of colors, and she spotted the white one, as if there was a lighted arrow pointing directly at it.

"Is this what you were looking for, Ma'am," asked the young girl.

"Yes, that's exactly what I was looking for. You're a lifesaver. Thank you."

"My pleasure. Is there anything else I can help you with?"

Eva snatched the scarf and took off.

She looked back at the girl standing there and said, "Nope, I'm good."

Once she was back in her car, she put everything she needed into one bag. She sat there mentally putting it all together in her mind.

She reached under the seat and pulled out a large book that looked to be a hundred years or so old. The pages were yellowed, frail, and the binding looked rough, but it was in a beautiful brown leather hardcover. There was no title on the front, but once she opened it, words and pictures in black cursory ink filled the pages. Words to some may seem Greek, but she knew what they meant, even if it had been twenty plus years since she'd set eyes on it.

Her family's crafting filled the pages of this book. Just touching it freaked Eva out a little. She had packed this book away in the wooded trunk a long time ago and never once looked for it.

Eva's phone began to chirp, and she glanced down to see who it was.

"Hi Sweetheart, how are you?" she asked.

"Hungry. Where are you," her husband laughed.

"You're always hungry, and you know how to cook. I am out shopping and then I'll be home."

She purposely didn't mention what she was out shopping for, because she didn't want to get him involved. The less Kris knew the better, especially if something went South.

"Okay, I guess I'll start making dinner. The natives are getting restless here. Be careful, and don't put me into too much debt okay," he said, only half joking.

Eva just laughed, told him she loved him and hung up. She could tell that he knew tonight was the night. He just didn't say it outloud.

Eva sat in silence and took a few deep breaths. Her nerves were starting to pick up just a little. She knew she had to get them under control if she had any chance in hell if she was going to make this to work.

As she made her way back to town, she listened to her music, which always seemed to calm her.

Even growing up, Eva surrounded herself with music. It had a peaceful calming effect on her, so when she gets stressed, the first thing she does is crank up the tunes. Tonight was one of those nights. Linkin Park was blaring through the speakers of her BMW, and she was jamming right along with them.

As she got closer to town, she was reaching her zen mood, and her thoughts were looking up. From the parking lot, it looked as though everyone had gone home for the night.

She grabbed her bag of goodies, locked her car door, and made her way to the shop. She was careful not to attract any undue attention. She had a key to the alley gate, so she didn't even have to go to the front door. The front entrance would have too much foot traffic, and she didn't want to risk being seen.

It was darker in the alley than she remembered, but she wasn't used to being back there at night. The feel made it kind of spooky.   It also brought back the image of all the blood that had drained from Trudy Baylor.

Her body gave a slight shake, but she continued on.

With a dimly lit flashlight in hand, she walked slowly through the narrow corridor, and made her way to the fire escape where it all happened.

The air still smelled of death, decay and dried blood. The scent of wet rust, salt and iron wafted through the air. The clean up crew hadn't been able to fully clean the blood stains off the concrete and iron stairwell. Remnants of what occurred still lingered.

Looking around the alley, Eva made sure no one could see her from the alley entrance. She looked up toward the roof, and knew no one used that entrance during the evening. That was only used by businesses around there, and it was only used during the day. Today most businesses had their employees use the front entrance. They wanted to make them feel safer.

She placed her bag on the ground, and emptied the contents one item at a time, taking in each item.

Chrissy's life was on the line now, and if she could do something to help her, she'd do it.

Deep down Eva knew she didn't kill Trudy, but now she had to use her one gift that she swore she'd never use again.

This spell would at least give them a 90% successful way to see who the real killer was. Once she got the answers she was looking for, by performing the spell, she would look for the real evidence to prove it to the police.

The first thing Eva needed to do was to perform a protection spell around her. She poured some white baking powder into a circle around the area where Trudy had been laying. She then placed the four white candles equally spaced around the outer part of the circle.

Eva wrapped the white silk scarf around her shoulders and began chanting, "In the shadows, evils hide, ready to draw me from loves side, but with your help I shall be strong, banish all that do me wrong. Send them away, send them astray, never again to pass my way. So mote it be."

Eva took a deep breath, and swooshed the air back out quickly, and opened her eyes.

Eva entered the circle she made with the powder and formed another circle inside that, with salt. Stepping outside the circle, she grabbed the jar of pigs blood and began pouring it into the middle of the second circle.

The sight was almost too much for her to handle, and she choked back the bile that had formed in her throat. She continued on with her task. Once the pig's blood was poured, she placed one more white candle into the middle of the blood. She lit each candle, saving the middle one for last.

"This better work, pigs blood Is not too appetizing to work with."

She stood back and gazed down at the circles before her, she gripped the white scarf a little tighter to her. She closed her eyes, concentrated and tilted her head to the sky. She began the spell in a low tone.

"Power of the witches rise, coarse unseen across the skies, take me back to where I'll find what I wish in place in time."

Eva opened her eyes. Her hair started to blow around her face. She looked into the pool of blood and the flame of the candle and chanted, "I wish to see the events that unfolded twenty-four hours ago, bad or good, let me see, so mote it be."

The blood pool started to ripple, changing colors from red to black, then an image started to form. The pool of blood turned into a TV screen. It was the alley, right where she was standing, but it was empty. Nothing but the fire escape stairs was showing.

She heard a noise in the distance and it caught her attention. She thought someone was coming, until she noticed the noise was coming from the scene inside the pool of blood. It wasn't Trudy though; it was a male figure, the back of a male figure.

"Oh come on, turn around, let me see your face," she said to herself.

The image turned around, as If hearing her request, but she still couldn't make out who it was. He was coming through the gate to the alley, where only people with keys could get in.

Those keys were only given to business owners, and employees. Anyone can leave out the gate from the alley, but it locks automatically when the door is shut.

This was making no sense to Eva, and she was getting frustrated not being able to see the males face.

Again, she heard another noise in the direction of the gate into the alley.

"Oh my God, it's Trudy," she whispered, as her hands went to cover her mouth.

What she heard next, was not what she expected.

"Gerard, why did you ask me to meet you here? I thought we were going to discuss your new business proposition," Trudy asked, confused.

"Oh we will Trudy, I just wanted to show you a possible location for the new place."

"But, this is where A Cut Above is located. They're not selling or going out of business. I would know if they were in trouble," she said snidely.

She continued to walk toward the back of the alley, where the fire escape was.

Gerard walked closer to her and said, "You know Trudy, you were one of my Mom's oldest clients, and she was truly hurt when you started to go to Chrissy. You even had the gall to follow her to her new place here. She felt truly betrayed," Gerard said. His tone was menacing.

"It's been years since I've gone to your Mother, Gerard. It was nothing personal, but Chrissy listened to me and did what I wanted.

68

"You can't say it wasn't personal Trudy. You and mother were best friends. Is that how you treat your friends," he chided her.

"If you must know the truth Gerard, your mother betrayed me and tried to ruin my marriage. She came on to Troy at our country home, while everyone was there for our annual Fall Fest weekend, five years ago. He turned her down, of course, but she told everyone that he had come on to her. It took months for our reputation to get back into good standing with our friends and business partners. So, I guess it was personal, but it was business, too."

Throughout her confession, Gerard had noticeably inched closer to Trudy. His moves were slight, but calculated.

Watching the scene playing out, as if she were watching a daytime soap opera, Eva's eyes grew bigger and her mouth dropped open. A wrinkle formed between her brows, knowing the end was coming soon.

"Gerard! You sick son of a bitch, of course it was you," she spit out.

As she continued to watch everything unfold, she started to get a little nauseous. She knew she had to let it play out completely, to make absolutely sure he did it.

A scream lifted Eva out of her thought process, and she noticed he had pushed Trudy against the brick wall. She ducked quickly, and swerved over towards the stairwell. She started to climb the stairs. He reached in his back pocket, and pulled out a pair of shiny silver shears, flipping them completely open with one hand. He grabbed the back of Trudy's coat with the other. She had mis-stepped and fell down a step, but Gerard was younger and stronger. He had her in a choke hold, with one arm around her neck and shoulders, the other poised with the open shears. It happened so fast, Eva fell back on her butt, and it was as if she were there that night.

Gerard made one quick motion with the shears in his hand and scalped Trudy from her forehead, to the back of her neck. He made the same motion at least five more times, until her hair and the skin that surrounded it, were gone. Nothing but her boney skull was left on her head.

He let her body drop onto the stairs, and turned her around so she was face to face with her monster. He said, "Now that's a beautiful haircut, Trudy."

He made one last swipe across her neck, where he caught her jugular, and she was done.

He smiled and swiped a finger down the shear. He held up his finger, blood dripping from it and he put it to his mouth and licked it. His eyes closed, and he let out a delicious sounding sigh. He made it look like he had just licked frosting from a bowl.

Gerard looked around, then put his shears back into his pocket. He proceeded down the alley and walked out the gate. He made sure it was wiped down and locked on his way out.

Eva looked back at the scene, trying not to dry heave. It was honed in on Trudy's face, covered in blood. There were only gurgling sounds coming from her, as she lay bleeding out.

This was it, this is what she needed to find out. Relief flooded through her as she realized it wasn't Chrissy who killed her, or any of the other girls.

This was good news, but now she had to prove it.

The first thing she had to do now, was end the spell.

Still wrapped in the protection of her scarf and the protection spell, she closed her eyes. She raised her head to the sky, clasping her hands tightly together, and said, "Power of the witches rise, coarse unseen across the skies, bring me back to the here and now. I wish to be in the present, no harm, no foul, let me be, so mote it be."

Looking at her surroundings, it looked as if nothing had ever taken place. Everything was back to normal. The salt, powder and blood were completely absorbed into the earth. The candles lay in their positions where she had placed them.

Eva sat back against the wall for a second, to catch her breath. She sat with her head in her hands, and tears streaming down her face. Seeing Trudy's face, again. It had been different from the moment she had found her yesterday morning. Now she had the image of Trudy's terrifying last moments to haunt her.

She picked up the used candles, placed them back in her bag, and walked toward the gate entrance. She looked out into the dark night, turning her head to the right and then to the left. She was making sure no one would see her coming out of the alley so late.

Looking at her watch, she noticed that only twenty minutes had passed, which was a lot less time than she had thought. To her, it felt like hours.

Eva was exhausted, and wanted to get back to the safety of her home and her family. She drove in silence, with no music, just meditative breathing.

She had no idea how she was going to make people believe her about Gerard. She knew one thing, she had to tell someone what she saw, and she knew that someone was going to be Kris. He already knew what she was up to tonight.

Chapter 13

She arrived home to find dinner on the table. The kids were sitting there behaving, and Kris was smiling at her. He gave her a knowing nod that said he was glad that she got home safely.

It was quite a bit later than their normal dinner time. She pushed the last thirty minutes deep inside and smiled at them. After she put her coat and purse away, she joined her family and ate dinner in peace. Surprised that she could even stomach food right now, amazed her. The vibe in her safe and cozy house was the reason she could sit and enjoy her meal.

Kris and Eva stood at the sink, washing dishes when Kris turned to her and asked, "so, did it work?"

Eva stood stock still, surprise showing on her face. She had already assumed he knew where she had been, but she still asked, "What?"

"Eva, you never could hide anything from me, it is written all over your face," he said, laughing.

Eva wrapped her arms around him tight, and hugged him for all he was worth.

"It did work, and it was just as horrible as I had imagined," she confessed.

He pulled her away, and stood staring down at her.

"You're serious? It worked? You saw Trudy Baylor's murder as it was taking place, and who did it?"

Kris stared in disbelief. He thought it was all hocus-pocus, that she could actually have that kind of power. I mean, he knew of her past, but this, this was not normal. He didn't know what to make of this new information. All along he thought it would never have worked, that it would have been for nothing, and she'd stop thinking about using her witchcraft to find things out. Deep down he'd prayed it wouldn't work. Now there was no denying it, his wife was a witch.

Kris did his best to compose himself, before asking the inevitable.

Eva was still holding onto him. In her ear, he whispered, "I know I am going to regret this but, what did you see?"

She buried her face deeper into his chest. She relayed the whole scene to him and how she was able to concoct everything.

She looked up into his eyes and studied his face. He was processing all this new information. Kris' face went from stunned, to angry, but most of all, fear for his wife.

"Eva, what if someone saw you, or worse yet, what if Gerard had come back to the scene of the crime?"

Worry took over, and she couldn't blame him, she was pretty reckless with what she did. She wasn't thinking about all the possibilities of things going wrong, she did what she had to do.

She threw her hands into the air in frustration, "Now that I know the truth, what do I do with his information? It's not like I can just go to Lt. Murphy and tell him this, let alone tell him how I found out. They'd lock me up, for sure."

Kris grabbed her by the hands, and tried to calm her, "Well, we'll just have to think of something else; find evidence that he did it. I wonder if he threw the shears away? If we could find those, and his fingerprints are on them, we wouldn't have to explain how you knew he did it."

"What is this "we" stuff? You can't get involved, I won't let you." She was adamant.

"Hey, you are not doing this by yourself. You already went behind my back and performed the spell without telling me when you were going to do it."

He had reigned in his temper for the most part, but he still wasn't happy about what she did. He was still dealing with the knowledge that she could actually do it. Kris wasn't sure how he felt about that yet. He knew one thing though, and that was she was not doing any more of this snooping business without him.

"I'm putting my foot down, Eva. We are doing this together, and you will not argue with me. You were lucky tonight, but who knows what could have happened. I am not willing to take that chance."

Hurt and worry filled his eyes. Eva could see that she had made a mistake by not telling him that she was going ahead with her plan tonight.

"I'm sorry I didn't tell you earlier, I hope you can forgive me. I didn't want you to get into trouble, if something had happened."

"I understand that, but please don't leave me out anymore, okay?"

"Okay, I will let you in on everything I intend to do, from now on."

Unfortunately, Eva wasn't so sure she could keep that promise, but she would try.

Eva lay in bed, tossing and turning all night. She couldn't come up with a plan to get anywhere near Gerard. A plan that wouldn't look suspicious, or just plain odd anyway.

Looking at the bedside clock, it was 3:30 am, and she was nowhere near being able to fall asleep. Every time she closed her eyes, the scene from tonight would start playing over and over again. She would see the crazed look in his eyes, and the pleading, terrified look on Trudy's face as the life drained from her body.

Chapter 14

Tensions were running high in the shop this morning. Chrissy had called in to say that she had cancelled all her appointments that day. Shannon was a little more than concerned. Eva was trying to be her normal jovial self, but with the new revelations of last night and no sleep, it was hard.

Sarah Atkins is another owner of A Cut Above. She had been absent from the mayhem the last few days, due to taking care of her ailing mother. She's one of five kids in her family, and they all try to take turns caring for her. Sarah is in her fifties, never married, and no kids, but she loves her fur babies. She is one who does not like change, and is very good at what she does. She is also a pretty savvy business woman, as well as crafty. Delaware has been her forever home, and she'll never move. So this incident might just do her in.

Eva spotted Sarah coming through the back entrance that day, which meant she had driven to work. Normally she walks, since she lives in the downtown area. She owns a moderately sized home, that is cute as a button. It's a saltbox home with a decorative door, and a different holiday wreath adorns her front door all year round.

"How's your mom doing Sarah?" Eva questioned.

"She's a tough old bird, she's hanging in there. She is always asking for crazy food requests." She laughed a little, thinking about it.

"She is lucky to have all of you helping out."

"Hey, where's Chrissy," she asked.

"She called all her clients and cancelled them today. I'm worried about her. She's taking this all so hard, and I know she had nothing to with Trudy's murder."

"Well if you ask me, the old bat deserved what she got. She has been nothing but a bitch to everyone in town, and is only out for herself."

"Sarah! I had no idea you felt that way about Trudy." Eva said, surprised.

"Oh please, she only married Troy for his money. She only ever cared about her social status in this town. Guarantee you, not many will miss her."

Sarah had made her feelings about the dearly departed quite clear. If Eva hadn't already seen who killed her, she may have suspected Sarah. As it was, Sarah wasn't one to mince words, she has no filter. She just often says what she thinks. It's one of the many reasons most of the older ladies in town choose to go to her. They were from an era that has strong opinions about things. Sarah will let them have it, if she doesn't agree with them, or if she thinks they are out of line.

The phones in the salon were ringing at a higher volume than usual, which was good. Unfortunately most of them had been either newspaper reporters or television stations wanting to interview the girls about the incident. None of them were interested in giving any type of public statement. Outside there were news trucks camped out on the street, but no one had the nerve to come in yet.

"Do you see those vans out there?" Shannon had observed.

"Yeah, they were there when I came in." Eva said.

"And Chrissy is home hiding so we can deal with them."

"I don't necessarily think she's hiding. I mean, she has been named the number one suspect. I think she's scared." Eva explained. "You know she had nothing to do with it, right?"

"Eva, I know you try to find the good in everyone, but this isn't just a simple who took my hairspray situation."

Chrissy had a tendency to "borrow" stuff from the other stylists at times, and not return them. This was murder, and Eva knew she was right about Chrissy not having anything to do with it, and she was getting mad.

"Shannon, I know she didn't have anything to do with Trudy's damn murder!"

"Honey, you don't have to yell at me. I don't like your tone, where is this coming from?"

"I'm sorry, I didn't sleep very well last night and I am a little on edge."

"I see that, but you don't have to take it out on me."

Eva was having a real hard time not conveying the truth to Shannon, just to shut her up. She kept the truth to herself because how would she explain her knowledge of knowing Chrissy didn't commit the murder. That's one explanation she wasn't ready to deal with yet, so she dropped it and went back to the front desk. She tried concentrating on doing some minor accounting duties.

That task lasted all of fifteen minutes, when the phone rang again and this time it wasn't a client, or news outlet.

Eva had picked up the phone and with her happy voice said, "A Cut Above, how can I help you?"

The other end was silent for a second, and she thought it was going to be a telemarketer, but then a distorted voice began speaking, sounding almost like a robocall.

"Chrissy will go down, and she will take all of you with her, I will make sure of it. A Cut Above is over. Oh, and Eva, I know."

And there was a loud click, and that was it. Eva sat there speechless. She knew it was him, but she couldn't tell anyone, not yet anyway.

"Eva, you look like you just saw a ghost, are you okay," Sarah asked.

"I'm not sure. That call I just took, sounded like a robot, but it wasn't.   I think they used a distortion box. The gist of it was, Chrissy and this salon is going down."

80

She purposely left out the last bit of the conversation. She wasn't sure where she fit into this.

Sarah looked at Eva in disbelief and started laughing.

"Oh Eva, your imagination is definitely working overtime sweetheart."

"I'm serious, that's what the caller said," she replied defensively.

"Okay, okay. What was the phone number? Can you pull it up, again? We'll call it back and see who answers."

"Good idea!"

She found the last call that came in, and they hit call on the handset. They waited for the person to answer, but a message came on saying, "this number is no longer in service."

The women both looked at each other confused. Sarah took the phone and tried it again, with the same response.

"How the hell can it be no longer in service, when not even a minute ago it was calling here," she asked.

"I don't know, but don't you think I should call someone? Maybe I should call Lt. Murphy?"

"I guess it wouldn't hurt. Maybe they can trace the call or something."

Eva immediately called over to Delaware's finest and requested to speak with Lt. Murphy.

"This is Murphy."

"Lieutenant Murphy, this is Eva St.Claire over at A Cut Above Salon. I have a question for you."

"How can I help you Ms. St.Claire?" He seemed a little annoyed.

"I don't know if this means anything, but we just received a call from a phone number, saying they were going to take Chrissy and the whole salon down. Unfortunately the voice on the other end was pretty scrambled. We tried to call the number back, but it said it was no longer in service. Is there any way you can look it up or trace the call?"

Lt. Murphy seemed to perk up a bit and replied quickly, "don't do anything else, I'm on my way over."

Eva hung up, even more confused by the sudden rush for him to come to the salon. She shrugged it off, and let the girls know he was coming.

Not even ten minutes later, the lieutenant walked in, all business and not in a friendly mood. "Ms. St. Claire, may I see the phone number that had called?"

Eva brought up the number on the phone's handset and handed it to him. She wouldn't forget it, not for a long time.

Lt. Murphy seemed to be texting someone the phone number, so she waited patiently while he was doing his job. She guessed he was having the number run or traced, or whatever it is they do. Maybe they could find out who owned the number.

"Ms. St.Claire?"

"Eva, please."

"Okay, Eva. Did you happen to recognize the voice on the other end of the call? Was it male or female?"

Eva's face turned up in frustration. "Honestly sir, like I said, the caller could have been a robot for all I know. It sounded all wacky and computer like."

Lt. Murphy was getting annoyed by the minute. "Of course it was." He replied with disdain in his voice.

"What does that mean?"

"It means, Mrs. Cramer received a similar call yesterday, and came to me. SHe wanted to see if I could find out the same thing. We found out that it was a burner phone that had been used, and anyone can buy those. They can also buy a distortion box. She could have easily had someone call and make it out to be her as the victim, to take suspicion off of her. By the way, is Mrs. Cramer here, I'd like to talk to her."

Eva was dumbfounded, and just blinked at his accusations and questions. She had almost forgotten that Chrissy wasn't there.

He tapped her shoulder, "Ms. St.Claire?"

Startled, she jumped at his sudden touch. He recoiled in response.

"Are you okay?"

"Yes, yes I'm fine. Umm, Chrissy is out of the shop today. Is there something I can help you with?"

A notification sounded from his phone and he had received a text. Lt. Murphy looked down at his phone in mild disgust, but tried to hide it. He didn't want to give too much away. He just looked at Eva in disappointment.

"Well, again the number was from a burner cell, and can't be traced. Now with Mrs. Cramer not being here today, it doesn't look good for her right now."

The officer turned to leave, and Eva piped up, a little loud, "But I know she didn't kill Trudy!"

He turned around slowly, looking down at her. She shrank in on herself. He stared at her, trying to read her face, and her mannerisms, but wasn't getting any real tells.

"Excuse me? How do you know she had nothing to with Mrs. Baylor's murder?"

By this time, everyone's eyes were on Eva. She could feel the heat rising up in her body, and the overwhelming looks and the chagrined faces of the patrons that were in the shop, made her feel embarrassed.

Covering herself, she replied quickly, "I just know she couldn't have done this. Chrissy couldn't hurt a fly."

"It's hard to believe, when all the evidence is pointing to her, don't you think," he asked.

"What evidence? Did you find the murder weapon?"

Anger was brewing throughout Murphy, he wasn't' prepared for the third degree he was getting from such a small woman.

"No, the murder weapon has not yet been found."

"Then what evidence, other than she was found here, and they had had a mild disagreement that day, do you have?"

Eva stood tall and proud at her observations, and she could tell Lt. Murphy was not happy at her line of questioning of his authority.

He had had enough of this, he was on his way to the door when Sarah yelled from the back of the room,

"You know, lieutenant there were a lot of people in this town who aren't too hurt by the fact that Trudy Baylor is dead."

He turned around, and walked in her direction. He stopped at her chair, looking her in the eye, and asked "Would you be one of those people?"

Sarah looked him straight in the eye and said, "yes, I am."

"What is your name," he questioned.

"Sarah Atkins, why?"

"You're one of the four owners, correct? Why had you not shown up yesterday, when everyone was notified to come to the shop?"

He was shooting from all angles, but Sarah didn't look the least bit upset or frazzled by the confrontation.

"And, where were you the night before last, Ms. Atkins?"

She was gearing up her retaliation, and started with question one, and kept going.

"First off, yes I am one of the four owners, two, I had my phone ringer set to silent, and the reason for that was I was taking care of my dying mother the last few days. As for the night in question, I reiterate, I was at my parents' house, taking care of my dying mother. If you need to check it out, I suggest you call the hospice nurse that was there half the night, along with me, as well as my siblings. If you need any phone numbers, I will be happy to provide them to you. Is there anything else?"

"Not at this time, no." He stood there glaring at her.

The look on his face was priceless. As he exited the shop, his face was beet red. Eva could have sworn she saw some smoke emanating from his large ears.

Everyone looked in Sarah's direction, and she just smiled and continued on with her work.

Eva sat back at her desk, and thought through all the information she'd learned as she was talking to Lt. Murphy. Chrissy had gone to him yesterday after receiving a call from an unknown source, as well. He hadn't believed her. It wasn't like her to lie or to even come up with something like that burner phone idea. And now, he still thought she was lying, even after the shop got a similar call, that ended up being from a burner cell as well. Her not being at work today, when he showed up, didn't help matters either.

Eva pretended to be busy at her computer, but she was just brainstorming about ways she could get Gerard to talk.

First things first though, she thought. Eva needed to talk to Chrissy, and the sooner the better.

Before leaving for the day, Eva called Chrissy, but got her voice mail. After she left her a message that she had earmarked "Urgent", she waited to see if she'd call before she took off for home.

It wasn't even five minutes that had passed, and Eva's phone was ringing. Thankfully it was Chrissy.

"Chrissy how are you," she asked, as she picked up the phone.

"I'm hunky-dory hon, what's up?" She sounded drunk, but with Chrissy, you just never knew sometimes.

"Having you been drinking?"

"I may have had a glass of wine, or four. Why?"

"I was worried about you, and I wanted to check in. Also, I'd like to come over and talk to you about something. Are you available for a few minutes?"

"You're quitting on me aren't you?"

"What? No!"

"It's okay, I don't blame you. I'd want to quit, too, if I'd worked for me. Bad press will be floating around town soon."

Eva thought Chrissy sounded more down than she'd ever thought.

"We haven't heard of any horrible press going around, but I do need to chat with you about something that can't wait. Can I stop by?"

"Sure, and bring a bottle of Chardonnay while you're at it. Thanks." And she was gone.

Eva sat there shaking her head.   She was thinking that had to be the weirdest conversation she'd ever had with her, thus far.

The whole way over to Chrissy's house, Eva was rehearsing the whole speech in her head.   She was thinking how she was going to tell her that she knew she didn't kill Trudy, but she also knew who did.

"Maybe it's best that she's drunk."

Chapter 15

Eva stopped at Vito's Wine Bar on her way to Chrissy's. She purchased a really tasty Kendall Jackson Chardonnay that she knew was Chrissy's favorite.

She pulled into the neighborhood where the Cramer's resided. She couldn't help noticing that there were a couple of news vans camped out a house or two away from hers.

"Vulture's!"

She parked her car, and grabbed the bag that held the wine. She headed toward the front door, all while keeping an eye on the van's. She noticed them looking at her, so she lifted her hands in the air, as if to say, "Can I help you?"

She thought she'd piss them off and take their picture with her phone camera, as well. She laughed as she continued to the front porch, and rang the bell. There was movement and some sort of thump. That made Eva's eyebrows go up.

"Eva!! You're here, and you brought me a gift, that's so sweet. You brought me a going away gift."

"Where are you going Chrissy," Eva asked.

"Up the river from the sounds of it. You're here to tell me you're quitting, aren't you?"

"No. I told you I'm not going anywhere. I needed to talk to you about something. You're not going to go to jail. I know you didn't kill Trudy."

She waited patiently while she let that sink in.

Even though she was pretty inebriated, Chrissy looked to Eva with hope in her eyes and a little confusion.

"You're the only one in town who doesn't think that. I mean, I know I didn't kill her and I think my family believes me, but even my clients are bailing on me."

She started to tear up, and Eva knew she had to tell her how she knew. She was also scared to tell her exactly how she obtained this information.

"I know who killed Trudy," she blurted out.

"What? Who? How?"

The one word questions just spilled out into a blob from Chrissy's mouth. Her eyes were curious, and almost looked to be sobering up.

"Yes. I know who killed her. It was Gerard, he did it. He was getting back at you for leaving, and taking Trudy with you. He was also getting back at Trudy, for leaving his mother."

Shock and confusion replaced the inebriation Chrissy had been feeling.

"What the hell? What a low down dirty, sick, twisted individual; why I outta cut his balls off and feed them to my cat," she ranted. "What kind of person does something like that? One client, one measly little client. Okay, maybe it was more like half of his clientele, but still, that's a little overboard. This doesn't make any sense, how did you find out that he did it?"

This was the question that Eva was dreading answering, from the moment she stepped into the door.

"The way I found out isn't important right now. We just need to find the evidence to prove it. I need to find his shears, or tell Lt. Murphy to get a search warrant for his salon. He can find them."

"No. First, you need to tell me how you know all this. I am not going to the police station again. They will think it is a phony story, like they did when I got a weird voicemail yesterday. They looked at me like I was crazy. They had people holding onto me, and watching me the whole time I was there. I'm not doing that again, not until you tell me how you know all this."

"Okay sit down, and I'll tell you everything," Eva said. She signaled for Chrissy to take a seat on the couch.

Looking weary and unsure, Chrissy sat down.

"Oh God, you weren't there were you? Please tell me you had nothing to do with it Eva."

"NO! Nothing like that. I had nothing to do with it, and I was not there. Last night however, I was there, in the alley, where it all happened. Before I tell you everything, I think I should let you know about my past. It hasn't been all sunshine and roses, okay. I came from a long line of..." she was hesitating. "Witches."

"Witches? Like Wicked witch of the North type or Glenda the Good Witch type," Chrissy asked.

"Well, my mother did some questionable things, but for the most part, they were good. Over twenty years ago

91

the dark magic took over my mother. My father, he was a good warlock, and still is, but I don't see my family much anymore. My sister and I had pretty much vowed never to use our magic, after our mother passed away. Last night was the first time I had performed any type of spell or used magic, in over twenty years."

"Wow..., just wow. I don't know what to say. Am I still drunk? Are you for real? I'm dreaming aren't I?"

Chrissy was apparently not buying into Eva's whole witchy powers story. Eva was regretting even mentioning it now, but she knew the truth. She had to make her believe it, too, especially if she was going to get herself off the suspect list.

"Listen, you don't have to believe me, but I know what I saw. If you want me to help you, you have to let me tell you everything."

Sitting up straighter and looking more sober, Chrissy put on a serious face when she looked in Eva's direction.

"You're right, but you have to see this from my perspective, too. I'm not used to people telling me their witches, and can see things that happened in my back alley."

"I get that, and I shouldn't have just blurted it out. I didn't know how else to tell you. Will you let me tell you everything I saw now?"

Chrissy sat, running her fingers through her hair. She let out a whoosh of air, out of frustration, but she inclined her head to Eva, to let her continue.

Eva started at the beginning, from when she arrived at the salon's back alley. She took her through every phase of the ritual, even the protection spell she had set around herself.

Chrissy just sat there taking it all in. She was shaking her head, not in disbelief, but in amazement. Once she was finished explaining, Eva looked to her for some kind of response, or sign that she understood what she was saying. Her expression was sort of blank, and she just stared at the wall.

"Chrissy!"

"What? Oh sorry, I was just in my own little bubble here. I heard what you said, and I am really trying to process it. I'm not sure what we can do with that information that will help me, though. You know the police won't believe any of that. They'll have us both put in the pink padded room," she laughed.

"I'll think of something, but at least for now, I hope this relieves some of your anxiety. We both know who did it. The problem now is, how do we prove it to the stuffed shirts."

"My family is so not going to believe this, when I tell them."

"Don't tell them anything yet. Do not tell them about me or any of this; not yet anyway."

Eva didn't want it going around that she was the town witch. Her life would be a living hell, if that were to happen. She remembered all too well, what the neighbors thought about her family while she was growing up. She was thankful it wasn't during the times of the Salem witch trials. She couldn't imagine putting her family through that kind of judgement. Her own kids don't even know of her past.

Chrissy stood in front of Eva, holding two glasses of the wine she had brought her. She handed her one of the glasses.

As Eva reached for her glass, Chrissy held hers up, and toasted. "Here's to putting a needle in that gay bastard's arm."

Eva choked on her first sip, but couldn't help laughing at the sentiment. It was obvious the mood in the room had changed, from gloom and doom, to hopeful and a bit vengeful.

"Mmmm, this wine is good. Now remember, don't tell anyone what I told you. I need to figure out a way to get physical evidence, before we can go to Lieutenant what's his name.

There may be a way for me to find it, but I don't want you involved in that," she said, cautiously.

"Oh no you don't, whatever this little idea is, I am going to be involved," Chrissy stated, adamantly. "I don't care if you have to resurrect your dead grandmother, I am going to be there to see it."

"Damn Chrissy. I don't think it would come to that, but I may have to brew up a little spell. I need to do some research first. I should really be getting home, Kris is probably wondering where I am."

"Does he know of your past, and what you did last night?"

"Yes, he knows, and he wasn't thrilled about me doing the spell on my own. The fewer people who see and know, the better. I'll see you at work tomorrow, right?"

"I'll be there. I haven't seen any cancellations on my books yet for tomorrow, thankfully."

Eva hugged her dear friend and boss goodnight, and set off for home. She had some research to do. She had to see if there was a spell or anything she could do to conjure up the location of those shears.

Chapter 16

Eva had been on the computer for most of the night searching the internet and her old books. She was looking for just the right spell, to find what she was looking for.

Some spells aren't as powerful, and are more for finding lost car keys or something trivial around the house. A spell to locate a murder weapon however, she was finding was a whole new ball of wax.

She hadn't even realized it was 4am, when Kris came into the office looking for her.

"Hey there you are, what are you still doing up?"

"I was just doing some research."

He walked over to her and came around to the chair she was hunched over in, and kissed the top of her head. He noticed the website she was on, and the books that surrounded her.

"Eva, what are you doing with all this information on spells?" He straightened up, looking her in the eyes.

"Now, don't get mad, but I think I can find a way to locate the shears that were used to murdered Trudy."

"I'm not mad, I'm worried. You promised you would never do magic again, especially after what happened to your Mother."

"This is not the type of magic my mother was into. She dealt dark magic, and it took her over. The power was too much for her, she let the darkness in, and it won.

I'm not looking into that magic; I'm trying to help, not hurt anyone. There's a difference, a difference my Mother didn't see."

As tears formed in her eyes, Eva's memories of her mother surfaced. She had been such a good witch, when Eva was much younger. She had returned from the Summer Solstice in 1986, and from then on Eva had noticed that her mother was changing. They were subtle at first, but then she got more and more into the dark magic. She was never the same. All she cared about was the money people would give her to perform spells, spells that were meant to harm people.

Even though she loved and missed her mother, she was more at peace knowing she was gone.

Kris saw the sadness in his wife's face.

"I don't want you to get hurt, that's all. I know you're nothing like your Mom." He assured her of that.

She looked up at him, with a slight smile.

"Thank you. I promise you, I will be careful. I told Chrissy everything when I went over to see her, so she knows. I told her not to tell anyone else anything I told her. We need to be able to find the weapon first, before anyone can know."

"Oh lord, what did she say when you told her?"

"She was surprised, but she listened to everything I had to say. I believe she was thankful, and almost relieved to know thatI found out who did it."

"I am going on record saying that I am not happy you're doing this. It makes me very nervous, but once you make your mind up to do something, I know there is nothing I can do or say, to stop you. Please be careful, whatever you do. I will help you if you need me."

He bent down and brushed a small kiss to her cheek, and went back to bed.

Eva was still reading one of her books when she noticed a glimmer of daylight coming in through the blind. She hadn't slept at all yet, and it was after six. The kids and Kris would be getting up for school and work soon, and she'd have to get ready for work, too.

After much research on the internet and looking through a few books, she believed she had found the one spell that covered everything she wanted to be able to do. It still made her cringe thinking about having to pull this part of her life back into the light, but it didn't look like there was any other way to prove Chrissy's innocence.

She knows she is different from her mother. Eva knew she would never go to the dark side of magic, but it still didn't make it any easier.

Eva had gone twenty plus years not once touching a bit of magic, or even thinking about it. In the last few days, her magic had consumed her.

"Ugh..."

Walking wearily to the kitchen, she got the coffee ready, breakfast started and heard footsteps above. Kris was apparently up, and waking the kids up for school. A lot of moaning and groaning was emanating from the second floor, and it kind of made her laugh.

"They think they're tired... I haven't even been to sleep yet."

Eva was checking her phone, and noticed she had missed a call. She had a voice message. She didn't recognize the number, but checked the voice mail. She couldn't understand the message at first, it was a little garbled.

"I saw you at Chrissy's house last night. She'll be going away for a long time. You shouldn't stick your little nose where it doesn't belong, Eva. I can do worse than what I did to Trudy, to you. She paid dearly for what she did, and I thoroughly enjoyed punishing her...

Eva sat stock still at her breakfast bar, hands shaking and utterly speechless.

"What the hell?"

She looked at her phone and pulled up the last number that called. She hit "call" and waited. Nothing, but a message saying this number is no longer in service.

She put her phone on the counter quickly as she could hear little footsteps on the stairs. One of the kids was ready and heading down.

Moving around the kitchen, Eva was getting lunches ready, and breakfasts on the table. Her morning routine was always the same, so it didn't require a lot of thought, which was good. She kept her poker face on, so no one would question her, especially Kris.

After everyone had left, Eva showered, dressed and got ready to leave for work. She cautiously looked out the windows now and then.   Feeling more vulnerable. Did Gerard know she was on to him?

She ran through the house putting protective spells on every door and window. Keeping her family safe from crazy was her number one priority.

Eva had gotten her lunch ready for work. She was on her way out to the garage door, when she stopped by her desk, and grabbed her .380, sliding it into her purse. She hadn't felt the need to carry that for a long time, even though Kris always wanted her to have it on her at all times.

Delaware was a rather safe town, for the most part.

Chapter 17

A Cut Above seemed to be on the busier side today, which was a good thing. It had slowed down quite a bit for a couple days. The girls had been pretty worried about business, after everything that happened. They didn't think their customers would want to get their hair done where a client had been murdered.

Shannon was manning the front desk when Eva came in.

"Eva! How are you? I am so happy to see you," she beamed.

"Hi Shannon. Is everything okay," she asked, skeptically.

"Oh God yes, we're just really busy already, and the phones have been ringing off the hook."

Relieved, Eva let out a whoosh air, she didn't even know she'd been holding in.

"You okay Eva?"

"Yeah, I'm good. Who is all here, today," she asked, changing the subject.

"From the schedule, it looks like everyone is here at some point today."

As Eva scanned the place, she saw Sarah, Georgia and Charlene were already here. Georgia and Charlene hadn't been around the last few days, to take in all the calamity. Georgia had a sick kid and Charlene had been on vacation.

Georgia Parks was a mom of two, divorced, and has had her share of bad times. Her ex is a sleaze and not very nice. Thankfully she met a super sweet guy, who treats her like a queen. She's athletic, mid-thirties, with longish brown highlighted hair, and she sort of has a boho style to her wardrobe. She is the color correction queen.

"How's Eric feeling, Georgia," Eva yelled.

"He's still coughing some, but getting better, thanks. How are you doing? I heard you saw quite a lot of excitement a couple days ago?"

"Oh, I'm fine. I just hope they find who did it soon."

Even though Eva already had the answer to that, she had to play it out.

"I heard Chrissy is a suspect, that's not true is it?"

"Well, I don't believe she did it, but right now she is their only lead, because of the little incident that happened."

Charlene was a petite woman in her early fifties, with two grown daughters, one married with a son and one in college. She looked over at Eva and said, "I don't know, Chrissy has a temper sometimes."

"Charlene, how could you even think she could be capable of doing something so disgusting and sick," Eva said.

"I've seen her get mad; it's not pretty."

"Okay Charlene, where were you the night of the murder?"

"I was babysitting my grandson Jackson, and he stayed overnight. I sure as hell didn't do it, I barely knew Trudy Marshall."

Charlene was getting her hair in a knot at the questioning, but Eva knew she didn't do it. It just ticked her off that some of them thought that Chrissy was capable of it.

Now that she knew the truth, she felt the very overwhelming sense of protecting her. She also had to protect herself, apparently.

It was around noon when Chrissy waltzed in, smiling like she hadn't a care in the world. It was a little too obvious she was happy and relieved, unlike the day before. Eva noticed her all too happy demeanor and shot her look, to take it down a notch. She instantly shrunk her smile and went to her station.

Eva was beginning to regret telling her anything.

Of course, Chelsea came over from the spa and rained on Chrissy's parade, soon after.

Chelsea went up to Chrissy, and in a low voice said, "Jerry called and said that Lt. Murphy may be coming in today, to take you in for more questioning. Did he call you?"

Chrissy looked horrified, she wasn't expecting that at all, not after what Eva had told her, just last night.

"No, I didn't get a call, but I haven't checked my cell today, either."

"Well, if they make a scene here today, by taking you in, in handcuffs, this is going to ruin our business. You know we have the two new girls starting this week. They came in last week to pick up their keys and sign their contracts. This doesn't look good, Chrissy. Please tell me you're innocent."

Chelsea was almost pleading with her.

"Of course I'm innocent! I didn't have anything to do with Trudy getting scalped. I wish you all would believe me. Eva believes me," she claimed. She looked over at her only ally, whose eyes were big, mouth wide open and shaking her head in agreement.

Chapter 18

The day seemed to drag on forever, until three o'clock rolled around. Lt. Murphy strolled in, with a smug look on his face.

"Can I help you," Eva asked.

As soon as the door opened every eye was on the front desk. Eva's face was turning a deep shade of red from her blood pressure and anxiety going through the roof.

Chrissy stood stock still. She was turning as white as a ghost.

"I'm here on official police business. I need to speak to one of the owners, Christine Cramer. Can you point me in her direction?" He asked her sternly.

"Umm... can you hold on for a moment. I'll see if the spa side is available for you to talk to her."

"I'd appreciate that, but really I'm just here to escort Mrs. Cramer over to the police station."

Eva wasn't completely surprised, after overhearing Chelsea earlier, but she didn't want a scene to unfold in the middle of the busy salon either.

"Can you follow me over the spa side anyway, I'd rather you not cause a spectacle in here, and embarrass Mrs. Cramer anymore than she already will be. I will bring her over momentarily. I promise."

She gave the man a pleading look, and thankfully he agreed to follow her over to the other side.

They walked by Chrissy's station, where Eva gave her a quick, but not so noticeable nod. She took him to the spa side of the salon as quickly as she could.

"Oh for the love," Shannon blurted out.

She took in Chrissy's deadpan face. She was in shock.

Thankfully no one was in the spa. Chelsea must have left for the day. Eva made sure the spa entrance door was locked, so no new clients would barge in. She excused herself and made her way back to Chrissy's station. She could see that she had regained some of her composure and was finishing her client.

Eva stopped at her station to let her know that she could take care of her client once she was finished.

"Did Lena need to reschedule, as well?" Eva smiled at Chrissy. "I can take care of it while you go speak to our guest waiting in the spa."

That would be great Eva, thank you."

The smile Chrissy gave didn't quite reach her eyes.

Eva walked her client up to the front desk. She looked over to where Chrissy was, still standing in front of her station, and gave her a knowing smile. She was trying to reassure her that everything was going to be okay. Chrissy just turned and solemnly headed for the spa, with her head down. It broke Eva's heart to see her friend going through.

Eva didn't know what else she could do at the time. She was truly afraid for her friend. She knew she couldn't prolong performing the finding spell any longer.

It was now or never. Tonight she would come back with all her paraphernalia, and pray it wasn't too late.

On the spa side, Lt. Murphy sat at one of the nail stations, waiting for Chrissy to get there. This was the part of his job he hated the most. He didn't know Mrs. Cramer all that well, but she had always seemed friendly and polite. The most he found on her was a few parking and speeding tickets, but they were all paid.

He sat and wondered what would make a person lose it so badly, to do something so heinous and grotesque to another human. As he was pondering this, his body shook from the memory of seeing Trudy's dead body.

Chrissy walked in and noticed the grim look on his face and wanted to bolt, but thought better of it. She knew she was innocent, and so did Eva.

The much larger man stood from where he was sitting, to approach her. She instinctively backed up a step.

"Mrs. Cramer, I really do not relish the prospect of having to bring you into the station again, but I have no choice. The DA is set on charging you in Trudy Marshall's murder."

He reached for the handcuffs that were attached to his back pocket, and started reciting, "You have the right to remain silent, you have the right to an attorney, if you can not afford one, one will be appointed to you..."

Chrissy was paralyzed with fear. The man kept droning on; the next thing she knew, he was turning her around and grabbing for her hand.

She whipped around, "I didn't Kill Trudy!! I swear, I'm being set up," she yelled.

She was trying to wiggle out of his grasp, but he was stronger than she was. He slapped on the cuffs fast, and was about to take her out through the salon, when Eva ran in. Her eyes were as big as saucers. She stood there dumbstruck and her mouth wasn't working. She just stared at the sight in front of her for a second. Finally her mouth opened, "What is going on in here," she exclaimed.

The officer explained what he was doing. He was starting to walk Chrissy towards the salon side, when Eva got him to stop before opening the door.

"Wait! Can't you take her out the alley? She does not need anymore stares and embarrassment."

"Fine. I'm parked on this end anyway," he said.

"Thank you. Now where are you taking her? I need to call our lawyer and tell him of this ridiculousness."

"Ma'am, this is not some joke. This is serious, and I would not be arresting Mrs. Cramer if I didn't believe otherwise. The CSI team uncovered fingerprints on the alley gate that were Mrs. Cramer's and Mrs. Marshall's, so now if you'll excuse me, I will be taking her to the police station and getting her booked. She will subsequently be arraigned, sometime today or tomorrow. If you'd like, you can have her lawyer meet her there."

"Wait... finger prints? That's all you have is finger prints? What about the weapon used? Where is that, did you find that? Of course her finger prints would be on that gate, this her business."

Pushing his way past Eva, Lt. Murphy hauled Chrissy out the back door, and they were gone. He had not given her any response to her questions.

Eva ran to the front desk, not even listening to the questions that were coming at her from all the other stylists; she picked up the phone and dialed Jerry Grimes, Attorney at Law. It rang at least four times before anyone answered. She explained the situation in as low of a voice as possible, so others wouldn't hear. However, Shannon was right next to her and heard everything. Eva hung up, and looked up at a stone faced Shannon, and shook her.

"Hey, get it together. Don't show everyone you're freaking out. Jerry is on his way to the station, and all we can do is wait. I need to call her husband."

Eva was very matter of fact, while Shannon was still locked in her place.

"I knew this was going to happen, Chrissy always gets herself in trouble with her mouth. She has no filter. I knew it, I just knew it, we're done for, we'll have to close up shop, and file for bankruptcy..." Shannon yammered on.

Eva gave her a smack in the arm to stop.

"Knock it off, people are watching. And, for your information, Chrissy did not kill Mrs. Marshall."

She looked down at her receptionist, annoyed and quite perturbed that she'd smacked her, and asked, "how do you know she didn't kill her? It's not like you were there."

Eva knew as soon as she said it, she was going to regret it. She couldn't tell her how she was so sure that Chrissy hadn't killed Trudy.

"I just know in my heart that she couldn't have done it," she claimed.

Shannon just rolled her eyes, and walked off.

"Very convincing Eva," she said to herself.

It had been at least three hours with no word on what was happening with Chrissy, when the phone rang. A muffled cartoon voice spoke, "She got what she deserved, and you better behave, or you'll be next." Click.

"What the hell?"

Eva was truly freaked out. She tried the number that had shown up on caller ID, but it said it was no longer in service.

"How does that happen so quick," she pondered.

She bent to check her purse, just to double check that her .380 was still in there. She let out a little sigh of relief when she saw it in there. She's never once had to use it, but she and her husband practiced enough that she was comfortable having it, and if she had to, she could use it.

The phone rang again, and Eva jumped out of her seat and let out a little squeal, causing people to look her way. She sat back down quickly and picked up the phone slowly, answering it with a shaky lilt to her voice. She was soon relieved when she heard Chrissy's voice. She was calling from home.

"How did you get home already?" She was relieved to hear her friend's voice.

"Jerry got the judge to grant me bail, since I'm not a flight risk, and I didn't do it!," she yelled. She was clearly frustrated.

"I don't want to upset you anymore than you already are, but I got another call from another crap cell phone." She skipped the part about them threatening her.

"Did you call the police? When did they call?"

"It was about ten or fifteen minutes ago. I didn't call the police, because they wouldn't be able to trace the call, since it was from a burner cell."

"Shit!"

"I'm sorry Chrissy. I am going to be heading home soon, to pick up the stuff I need to do the finding spell. I'll come back tonight to see if I can get anything to work."

"I want to be there when you do it," she said.

"I don't think that's a great idea."

"I don't care, I need to do something."

"What if they have someone watching your house, and following you? I can't risk getting caught doing magic."

Eva could tell Chrissy was thinking that over, and finally gave in to staying home.

"I promise I will let you know what I find out, as soon as I am done."

There was a few seconds of silence before Chrissy thanked her and hung up.

Eva headed home to pick up what she needed and would head back later, after everyone was gone.

Chapter 19

Eva had just returned to the salon, a little after 8:30pm. It was a new moon tonight, which meant it would be quite dark in the alley. That was a plus for her, she thought. The darker the better, so no one would see her.

She started to empty her bag; a mirror, an orange candle, a black candle and a small magnet.

She wasn't even sure this would work, but one had to take chances in order to help an innocent person clear their name.

As she was placing the items in the circle she heard a clunking noise coming from somewhere outside the alley. She instinctively located her purse that carried her .380, and was about to pull it, when the alley gate opened and a disheveled Chrissy ran towards her. She was huffing and puffing. The only way she knew it was her, was her voice, other than that, she never would have recognized her. She was dressed all in black, including a very long and very curly black wig and large reading glasses.

"What the crap Chrissy!? Why are you here? You should be at home. You know you could have been followed."

Catching her breath, she bent over, and Chrissy mumbled, "I ran here. I went out my backyard and through the back streets. No one saw me, and besides no one would recognize me in this get up."

"It still makes me nervous that you're here."

"I can help you."

Eva wasn't comfortable having an audience. She also knew Chrissy wouldn't listen to her if she told her to go home, now that she was here.

"Fine, but you have to listen to what I tell you, and don't distract me. I haven't done this spell thing in a long time."

"It seemed to work fine for you the other night, when you saw Gerard offing Trudy," she stated.

Eva continued to make up her circle of protection. She lit the black candle, to draw away negativity, then the orange candle, which was for luck. She needed a lot of luck right now.

Eva began to visualize the object she was searching for, which was the shears with blood and hair still attached to them. She pictured them in the mirror that was placed in the middle of the circle. Once she had the vision, she placed the magnet between the two candles.

"What's the magnet supposed to do, and what's with the mirror?" Chrissy interrupted her thought process.

Eva jumped, and gave her an annoying stare,

"Chrissy hush! You're going to make this more difficult than it has to be. Please, just stand against the brick wall, away from the circle, so we can get this done."

"Sorry."

Eva began her chanting of the incantation.

"By the wavering flame of this black light, grant me Gerard's shears a sight. By the power of this orange flame, give me luck to find the same. In this mirror the shears I see make the magnet draw them to me. So mote it be."

Eva repeated the spell two more times. Smoke began billowing around the circle. Both women stared in awe as the magnet started vibrating, and an image was starting to form on the mirror.

"Oh holy shit, what is happening," Chrissy asked in a low voice.

"It's locating the shears."

"I'll be damned."

"Shhh..."

"Sorry."

There they were, plain as day. The bloody shears, with a mess of hair still attached. From what it looked like, they were hidden in a box with bloody rubber gloves.

"What is that," Chrissy asked.

"It looks like everything we need to find is put away in some box. Where this box is, I have no idea. I may have to do this whole thing over, but this time I need to visualize this box. Do you see any remarkable markings on it?"

They both crouched down closer to the mirror, to see if anything stood out on the box. Chrissy was the first to notice something in the corner of the box. She knew exactly what box that was. She turned a shade of white that made Eva take notice.

"What are you seeing Chrissy?"

She bolted upright, and started pacing.

"What is it?!"

"I know that box. I gave it to Alice for Christmas one year. She collects antique wooden boxes, with velvet interiors. This specific box had a gold pin nailed into the interior. The gold pin had a small rhinestone in it. Look at the far corner," she pointed.

"So, you gave this specific box to Alice? Why would he have it?"

"I don't know, but it seems fitting don't you think?"

"He has a twisted sense of humor," Eva said.

"Yea, you don't know the half of it."

That took Eva a little by surprise, but didn't ask her to elaborate on it. They didn't have time for that, if she wanted to find where this box was located.

"I really need to try this spell again. Do you think he could have taken the box from his mother and then put it back, because he thought no one would look there?"

"It's possible, I guess."

Eva's thought process was trying to see if she could somehow make the box appear smaller, so they could see the surrounding environment. She was hoping it would give them an idea of whether it was back at Alice's house, or not.

"You've been inside Alice's house, right?" She asked.

"Oh yes, many times. She would have the salon Christmas parties there, why?"

"I'm hoping if we get a better picture of the box this time around, you'll be able to tell me if it is in her house, or not."

Chrissy looked over at Eva like she was crazy. Eva thought maybe she was, but she knew she still had to at least try this one more time.

"Okay, I'm going to blow out the candles, and restart the process, but this time, I'm going to put that box in the forefront of my mind."

Chrissy just stared down at her and said "by all means, have it."

Eva gave her partner a snarky look, but didn't reply.

Eva re-lit the candles, placed the mirror and the magnet back where she had them before, in between the candles. She repeated the spell three times, as she had before. Again, the area around the mirror and magnet had smoke billowing around it, making both women step back.

Chrissy was the first to notice that the scene didn't look as it had the last time. This time a different image was starting to take place in the mirror. They both took a step closer to the mirror.

Chrissy gasped in recognition at where it was showing the box being located.

"What? You know where this is?" Eva asked.

Chrissy's eyes went wide. "Yes, I know exactly where that is, but we'll never be able to get the box," she stated.

"Why, where is this?" Eva asked, with alarm in her voice.

"It's in the basement, or what we used to call the dungeon space, below the salon. There's no way we'll be able to get the evidence out of there."

Eva saw the panic in Chrissy's face, and she felt a little defeated. She would still try to think of a way to get that box out of there.

"Is there a reason you just called it the dungeon space?" Eva asked hesitantly.

Chrissy looked at Eva, she was stalling. Eva was growing more and more intrigued about the reason she called it what she had.

"It's... just such an old building, it was over a hundred years old and built in the 1800's. There were things down there that always made me kind of cringe. I thought they were just left behind from the 1800's, but now I'm not so sure. Now that I know what a sadistic person Gerard really is, those things could be his for all I know."

"What type of things were down there?" Eva couldn't help herself, she was always inquisitive.

"Rusty shackles hung from one of the walls, along with a really large table that had hooks drilled into the one end. Like someone could have been held down there, against their will. It always creeped me out to go down there." Her body shivered at the thought.

That wasn't exactly what Eva was picturing, but now it made a little more sense as to who they were dealing with. Eva thought she'd stow that away to think about later.

"I'll think of something, but in the meantime, you need to leave before someone happens to see us. Me, I'm not worried about, but what if someone spots you?"

"You're right, my family is probably wondering where I am by now."

"You didn't tell them that you were leaving?"

"No time, I just suited up and hightailed it out the back yard."

"Do you have your cell on you?"

"No. I didn't know if the cops were tracking me somehow."

"That's smart, actually. Go on home the same way you came down here, and text me, so I know you got home okay."

"Yes Mother," she said.

Eva just shook her head. "Go!"

Chrissy was headed out the gated door, with her hood up, and the strings pulled so it scrunched toward her face. Eva thought she resembled a vagrant from the streets with that crazy wig.

God, she hoped she wouldn't get noticed, even with that get up she was wearing.

Chapter 20

Eva cleaned up her supplies, put them back in her bag and headed into the salon from the back entrance. She just wanted to check on everything.

Everything looked normal, in the spa, so she headed toward the hair side. She noticed a small light on, and knew someone had to be there, because they always made sure that all lights were off, when the last person left.

She slowly opened the door to that side. She crept in quietly, and saw a figure at the front desk. It was a female figure, but one she was not familiar with.

Eva moved closer, and she was starting to make out who it might have been. Eva wasn't wanting to scare anyone, but Eva had every right being in here, this person didn't look familiar to her, so she decided speaking up was the only option for her. She had her gun ready, and she held it behind her back for the moment.

"Can I help you?" She spoke up loudly.

The figure jumped, and looked her way, completely taken back. Eva could see a little better the closer she got. It was their new nail tech, Gemma.

"Jesus, you scared the bejeezus out of me!"

"I'm sorry, but I could say the same about you. What are you doing here, this late at night, and on this side of the salon," Eva questioned. She didn't care how rude she may have sounded. It was a little too peculiar.

"Oh, I was just looking at this schedule app you all use here."

"What about it?"

"I wanted to get my hours put in, so I can start scheduling people."

She was quick, Eva would give her that.

She was dressed in all black. From her tight skinny jeans and black leather boots, to her black fitted turtleneck. Gemma was average height, and weight, but a stunning face. Her makeup was flawless, she had high cheekbones, full lips, but her shiny black hair was just in a ponytail. Not really matching the rest of her. An elegant cat burglar, Eva thought.

"You know you could have done that from your phone, or home computer right," Eva continued.

She knew she sounded downright rude, but she honestly didn't give a rats patooty, at the moment. She'd had enough surprises for one week.

"Oh, I didn't think about that. I guess that would make sense," she said as she started to gather her stuff together.

"So, I assume they gave you a key to the doors," she questioned.

"Um yeah, when I came in a couple weeks ago to sign my contract. I was just getting ready to leave; why are you here? It's Eva, right?"

Eva had a strange feeling about Gemma, but she wasn't sure why.

"I had left the bank deposit here, and need to take care of it, before coming in tomorrow. I live close, so I thought I'd come in and grab real quick."

Gemma was quick with answers, but Eva was better.

"Well, I'll let you get that, and I will see you again in a few days," Gemma said, as she was making her hasty retreat.

Eva heard the spa door close, and the lock tumble. She ran toward the front desk, her desk, for all intents and purposes, and searched for anything out of place.

Nothing stood out at first, but she noticed a sticky note in the wastebasket. She picked it up, but it only had a phone number on it. She thought it could be from anybody, but she knew that they didn't have sticky notes there.

She put the note on the desk, and she opened the computer to check for anything different. She noticed it was on Chrissy's schedule, for some reason.

She decided to open Gemma's schedule and it did indeed look like she had put in her hours and days that she is going to be working. Eva still had an uneasy feeling in the pit of her stomach. Eva thought something was off. Everything was off these days.

"I seriously need a drink," she decided. .

Once Eva locked up, she went to her car, which she had parked on the street, and not in the normal parking lot that they all parked in. She took notice of her surroundings and didn't see anything out of the ordinary, so she put her stuff into the trunk of her car and headed for home.

Still having a gnawing feeling in her stomach, she drove and pondered everything that happened tonight.

She hadn't practiced magic in twenty plus years, and she never thought she would be doing it ever again, but here she was. Now, a friend and co-worker knew what she could do. She saw it with her own eyes. Would Chrissy now look at her altogether differently, or would she just pretend she wasn't aware of her powers and her past? These were questions that plagued Eva the whole way home.

She glanced quickly into her rear view mirror. She noticed the person behind her had their brights on and was following a little too close for her comfort. She hated when drivers did that, it was annoying.

She drove a little longer and noticed nothing had changed, so she turned down a random street.

"Okay, let's test my theory." She said out loud, to no one.

She turned down a few other random streets that were close to her neighborhood and sure enough, the car was still behind her. It followed her at every turn, so she double backed and went around the block, and out the way she came in.

"Son of biscuit, I'm being followed."

She was debating calling the police, or would they think she was just paranoid?

She drove a little faster than the speed limit. She wanted to gauge whether or not they would speed up as well, to keep up to her, and sure enough, they matched her speed.

"Crap!"

Eva decided she better get her husband involved, or he'd wonder where she was. He had answered on the second ring.

"Kris, I was on my way home when I noticed a car following me. I've made several turns, and they did the same. I even tried speeding up, to see if they would try to keep up, and they did. What should I do? I don't want to lead them to our house"

"Where are you!?"

"I'm heading back toward downtown, again."

"Are you on William or Central going downtown," he asked. The concern in his voice was palpable.

"I'm heading down William Street"

"Okay, I'm leaving right now. I'll be just a couple minutes, if that, behind you. I want you to head to the Police Station parking lot. I'll meet you there. Can you tell what type of car it is that is following you?"

"I can't see much back there, they have their brights in my face."

He whispered an expletive that Eva barely heard, but got the gist of, and he was clearly angry.

"I'm turning onto Sandusky. I'll take Winter to Union. If they continue to follow my pattern, I'll turn into the Police Station parking lot."

"That works, but I'm not hanging up, so just continue, I'll be down there in a minute. And Eva?"

"Yeah?"

"Please tell me you have your gun with you."

"Of course. After the weirdness I've experienced this week, I am not going anywhere without it."

She could hear a small chuckle on the other end, and was glad she decided to call her husband.

"Okay, I'm on Sandusky, and they turned as well. Shit!"

"What?!"

"They just bumped my rear end."

"Eva, are you okay?"

"Yeah, I'm fine, just mad as hell, now."

"Change of plans; once you're on Union head to the ramp to route 23 and get on, and go as fast as you can. I'm going to head that way."

"Wait, what? You want me to try to outrun them?"

"You're a good driver Eva, you got this, and I'll be right there. I'm going to try to come in behind you, so I'm behind the driver that's following you. I want to pick up a license plate, or something."

Eva turned onto Union Street, and headed toward the ramp to get onto 23. Her hands were numb from the raging anxiety and anger that boiled in her. She hadn't used any turn signals, and wasn't going to before getting on the highway, either. She made a last minute left onto the ramp, and floored it. She had done that on purpose.

"Okay, I'm on route 23, and going about 90. Whoever it is back there, almost didn't make it, but they are catching up."

"Perfect, I just turned onto the ramp, I should be catching up to you soon."

If Eva didn't know better, she'd think her husband sounded almost excited about this.

She knew he'd catch up quick, he drove an Audi S5 for god sakes.

"I am almost to the light at Horseshoe Rd., where are you?"

"I believe I am about right behind you, but go into the left lane, so I know it's you
ahead of this car in front of me. If they follow, I'll know."

They did exactly what he thought they would do.

"Did you see that? Are you back there?"

"Yep, and we have a problem, there is no license plate on the car. It's black, and it's a sedan, but there are no other markings on it. Damn it!"

"What do I do now," she panicked.

"Give me a second, and don't you dare start to panic. You are stronger than that, Eva. I am right here, they just don't know it."

"Kris, what are you planning to do?"

"I might have to try to run them off the road, but you have to be ready to floor it, and take one of the streets, to make a u-turn, to head back toward town, got it?"

"Oh dear God, I'm not a NASCAR driver, Kris."

"Just tell me you understand," he yelled through the phone.

"I understand!"

"Good, now head to the right lane, they should follow."

She did as she was told, and of course, the idiot followed, as expected.

"There's a pretty big embankment up ahead; I'm going to persuade them over into it."

Nervous laughter on the other end caught him by surprise.

"What's so funny?"

"You're going to persuade them over? Sorry, it just sounded funny."

"Just get ready to move, I'm coming up on them now."

She could see him coming up on the left through her side mirror. They all had to be doing over 100 mph, now.

Just like that, Kris was moving in on them, and they jerked the wheel back towards him, they weren't going to go easy, that's for sure. One quick movement, and the other car miscalculated and swerved the wrong way, and went right down into the embankment.

Eva took off, and the first light she came to, she didn't even make a correct turn, just did a full on U turn and floored it back towards town.

She could see that her husband pulled off to the side of the road close to where the other car went over and screamed into the speaker phone, "what are you doing, let's go! Don't you dare get out of that car, Kris. I will turn around and come back, I mean it. Let's just go to the Police station, and tell them everything that happened. They can come out here. I'll hang up on you, and call them now."

She was starting to have a mild freak out, with the silence on the other end.

"Kris!"

"Okay fine, hang up and call 911, I'll be right behind you." He sounded irritated, but she didn't care about that right now.

Once on the phone with 911, she explained everything to the operator, who seemed genuinely interested, and possibly impressed, she wasn't sure. The operator assured her that they had someone on the way, immediately.

Before she even got to the exit ramp, she noted a police cruiser flying down the other side, no doubt heading to the scene. She called Kris back to let him know, and to see where he was.

"Should we head to the police station now," she asked.

"Absolutely.   They're going to check on whoever is in that car, and they'll have questions."

"You're right. Okay, I'll meet you there shortly. I'm just turning off the exit ramp."

"See you soon."

And he was gone.

Chapter 21

Eva was waiting in her car, in the station's parking lot, when Kris pulled up next to her. They looked at each other, and seemed to both breathe a sigh of relief, seeing that each other was okay. No worse for the wear, anyway.

She exited her car and walked over to Kris just as he was closing his door. She wrapped both arms around his waist.

"I don't ever want to do that again," she whispered into his chest.

He could tell she was on the verge of tears, but somehow she was holding it together.

"Hey, we did good, and it was kind of a rush, don't ya think?"

She just stared at the man like he was insane.

"No, that was not a rush, it was frightening."

He patted her back, trying to soothe her, hoping that she wouldn't lose it, right there in the parking lot.

"We really should go inside and see if we can speak to an officer."

"Trying to change the subject, are you?" She looked up at him, trying for a small smile.

"Was I that obvious?"

Shaking her head, she grabbed his hand, "let's get this over with, I'm tired."

They entered the building, and immediately saw Lt. Murphy coming down the hall. Eva recognized him right away. She was walking fast and almost barrelled right into him.

"Excuse me ma'am," he said.

He took in the small woman who nearly knocked him over, recognizing her.

"You're the lady from the salon, aren't you?"

"Yes sir, I'm Eva St.Claire, and this is my husband Kris. We need to talk to you, now."

"How can I help you, Mrs. St. Claire?"

"Can we talk in a more private area, by chance?"

"Sure, let's go to my office."

They walked up a flight of stairs, following him to a rather large, but fairly plain looking office. It had gray walls, neutral colored furniture, one smallish window, but no color, no family pictures, nothing. It was unadorned and very depressing. Eva took a cursory look, and was not impressed.

"So, what did you need to talk to me about? If this is about Christine Cramer, I can't tell you anything about the case."

"Well Sir, I was leaving the salon rather late tonight and was on my way home, when a car started following me. They had their brights on me the whole time."

Eva told him the whole story, blow-by-blow, and god love the man, he let her.

Once she finished, her husband intervened, "We called 911 as soon as it happened, so there should be one of your guys at the scene, now. You can check it out.

We'd like to know who was following her, because they also hit her back bumper."

He made a show of getting to his feet, and excused himself, saying he'd return soon.

"Where do you think he's going," she asked her husband.

"Probably calling the paddy wagon for us."

"That's not funny, Kris."

He chuckled, but took her hand, "he's probably checking with the 911 operators, or his officers on duty tonight, to see if we did indeed call 911. Also to see if they found anything at the embankment"

"Oh, yeah. You're probably right."

Her nerves were all but shot, and she was barely hanging on by a thread. She tried inhaling and exhaling slowly, to try to control her heightened anxiety. Eva closed her eyes.

Kris saw the Lieutenant coming their way, and nudged his wife to wake up. She jerked up, just as Murphy strode in, with an odd look on his face. He was very hard to read.

He sat down behind his bland old desk and stared at both of them, shaking his head.

"Well, you two are not going to believe this. When my officer got down to the embankment, where the car was, no one was inside."

Eva and Kris gave a look of disbelief. "You've got to be kidding me," Kris said.

The Lieutenant held his hand up, stopping him from talking further.

"Hold on. I have sent more officers out to that spot, to scour the surrounding areas, then we'll go from there."

"So what do we do in the meantime," Eva questioned.

"There was no license plate or any distinguishing marks on the car, so how are you going to track anything or anyone down, without that information. Can you check the VIN number on the car," Kris asked the Lieutenant. He was obviously getting annoyed that they hadn't turned up anything, so far.

"Yeah, my guy thought to check the VIN as well, and of course, it was missing."

"Of course." Kris said, a little too sarcastically.

Eva looked at the Lieutenant, ready to throat punch him, but she closed her eyes, took a deep breath, and asked, "so what do you suggest we do, now?"

"Mr. and Mrs. St.Claire, I'd suggest you go home, get some rest, and we will be in touch with you, as soon as we learn anything new."

As if they had the wind knocked out of them, they both went slack in their chairs.

"That's all you have to say to us, after everything we went through tonight," Kris yelled.

Eva sat up, grabbed her husband's arm, "Kris, it's fine, lets just go home."

"What? How can we just go home, as if nothing ever happened?"

She looked him in the eye, arched her left brow giving him a subtle hint as to what she was planning. He didn't like it, he knew that look, it was the same look she gave him the night she decided to open herself up to performing spells to help Chrissy. He didn't like it, and she knew it, but he stood, clasping his wife's hand, and headed for the door.

"Really, Mr. and Mrs. St.Claire, we will be in touch. I'm sorry for everything that has happened tonight. I hope you both can get some rest."

They both turned and nodded in his direction as they exited the office.

Once they reached the parking lot, Kris looked down at Eva, "I don't like it."

"What?"

"I know what you're planning on doing. You're going to go back to that embankment and try one of your spells. I think it's too dangerous."

She looked up at him, surprised at the accusation, then the corner of her mouth tipped up into a small grin.

"Damn, you can read me like a book."

"Don't forget it, either."

"We've obviously been together too long."

Kris just shook his head, opened his wife's car door for her, and let her sink into her seat. She looked up at him, she had yet to shut her door, when he leaned down to her. He gave her a peck on the lips.

"Let's just put it this way, if you're dead set on doing something where that car went down; I'm coming with you."

Well shit, she thought.   She hardly expected that to come out of his mouth. She did not want her husband to see that side of her. She had remained dormant for twenty years, and didn't even want to start using her magic again. Circumstances beyond her control, made that impossible.

She was afraid to have him see this side of her, he may look at her differently, if he sees what she is capable of.

Chapter 22

At home, Eva searched through her family's book of spells. She wasn't entirely sure what type of spell she was searching for, but it would more than likely smack her in the face when she found it.

Kris had made himself comfortable in the black leather sofa on the other side of her office. He'd made a pretty nice office for her in their extra room on the second floor.

Eva made sure it had bookshelves that lined the one wall. She loved books and read all the time. She loved mysteries, romances and thrillers. She read the occasional paranormal, but couldn't help thinking they were so far out there, that they weren't believable. Kris had his own selection of books he liked, too, but they were mostly Sci-fi, or technical in nature.

"Find what you're looking for yet?"

"Not yet, no."

She looked up to see her husband eyeing her warily. With a sigh, she said "I don't think you should be there with me, when I do the spell."

"Tough, I'm not letting you do this by yourself."

He didn't look at her like he was angry, but he was serious.

"I think I found it," she sat up straighter.

"Are you sure?"

"No, but this is the closest spell I've found yet, and I think it'll fit my needs. I'll need to get a few things before I do it, because I don't have all the items it requires, but I think this one will do."

"Where do you need to go to find these items?"

"Just the store. It's nothing they wouldn't have. I need sea salt, a white candle, a carving tool, which I think we have, along with milk, honey, flowers, and a small bowl. I just need to get a white candle and flowers. Everything else we have."

"So let's go then."

"Kris, I can do this myself, really."

"Why are you dead set against me going with you," he asked, questioning.

She put her head down, and stared at her fingers. She said in a whisper, "I don't want you to see this side of me."

He strode over to her, pulling her out of the chair she was sitting in, and gathered her into his arms.

"You think I'll see you in a different light, and that scares you, because you think I'll look at you differently, am I right?"

"Yes," she sniffled.

He hugged her tighter. "Nothing you do will ever change the way I feel about you, you should know that."

She pulled away and looked up at him, skeptical. She shook her head, not knowing how to phrase her fears properly.

"I don't want to take that risk."

"Honey, I'm not giving you a choice here."

"Always so smug, aren't you," she half laughed.

"Hey, you married me, remember?"

"Yeah, yeah. Let's go to the store and get this over with."

In the kitchen, Eva made the kids a snack, while she waited for her neighbor's daughter to come over and stay with them. She didn't think they'd be gone too long.

"You both behave for Jessie, okay?"

In unison, they both nodded at her.

"Why can't we go to the store with you and Dad," her oldest whined.

"Well, we have a few errands to run. We're not just going to the store, and I'm sure you'd rather stay home and play video games, than be with your boring parents."

"Fine, but can you at least bring home some kind of treat for us?

She rolled her eyes at her kids, "I'll try to remember."

As she was walking away, her oldest chimed in, "It's not that hard to remember, Mom."

The doorbell rang, saving her from further conversation with her kids. She walked towards the front door, to let Jessie in.

Jessie was a junior in high school. She was smart, and athletic, from playing volleyball the last four years for the school team. She was also very tall, standing at 5'10, her hair was always in a ponytail, she is such a cute girl.

Eva trusted her where her kids were concerned, and was thankful she was home tonight. It was late as it was, but this was an emergency.

"Hi Mrs. St.Claire!"

"Jessie, come on in, how are you?"

"Great! I got asked to the Homecoming dance by our star quarterback, Isaac earlier today." She was beaming.

"Wow, you go girl."

Laughing, she walked into the kitchen, where the kids were still seated at the breakfast bar, eating their snack.

"Hey guys!"

"Hey Jessie," they said simultaneously.

Kris came into the kitchen, where everyone had gathered.

"Are you ready to go, Eva?"

"Yes, let me just grab my purse. You guys be good, we shouldn't be gone too long."

"Later Mom!"

"They'll be fine, Mr. and Mrs. St.Clair."

Smiling back at her, they left through the garage door.

Chapter 23

Thankfully the store wasn't crowded. They were in and out in no time, with their bootie in hand. Eva had already put everything else she needed in her bag, before they'd left.

"Where do we need to go, for you to do this spell?"

"Back to the embankment, where the car had ended up. I'm thinking that would be the best place. I'm counting on the car still being there."

"Okay."

They rode in silence for most of the short trip up 23. Eva's hands were starting to shake, as her anxiety went up with each passing mile. Kris reached for her hand, and held it securely in his.

He looked over at her, smiled and said, "everything will be fine, ya know."

"I know. I'm just nervous."

They'd just passed Horseshoe Road, and she knew the embankment was just beyond this road.

"What if the car is gone, then what am I going to do?"

"Let's not worry about that just yet, okay?"

Easing over to the side of the road, and thankful it was black as pitch outside, they both got out. They peered over the embankment, and sure enough, the car was still there. Neither one of them knew whether to be grateful or not, that it was still there.

On one hand, Eva was hoping it wouldn't be, then she could just go home and curl up on the couch. She knew that wouldn't solve anything.

They made their way down the side of the steep embankment. She slid a couple of times, but got to the bottom safely.

Kris looked over at her and shrugged his shoulders. "Now what do we do?"

"We don't do anything. I will set everything up and you stay over there, and don't say a word."

"Ummm, okay."

She set her bag on the ground, and pulled the stuff she needed out of it and began setting it up, the way the spell instructed. She had everything written on a piece of paper, so she didn't have to bring the big book with her.

She made a makeshift altar with a large rock she'd found on the ground. She placed the new white candle on it. Her next step was to put the sea salt around the candle. She then took the small bowl she brought from home, and pulled the tops off the flowers they bought, and put them into the bowl, with the milk and honey. She lit the candle, stepped back, and glanced at her husband. He was taking it all in.

She started her incantation.

Au-set you incredible magician, your powers needed for this mission. With milk, honey and beautiful flowers, I ask for all your powers. Please find the soul that disappeared, and let my prayers be heard, let them be

found without a single wound, show me the path today,
and I will be on my way- Au-set you incredible magician,
your powers are needed for this mission.

She repeated the incantation thirteen more times, as was instructed in the book. Fog started to creep along the car, it got heavier each time she repeated the incantation.

She raised her hands up to the sky, her eyes closed. She pictured the car that followed her, zooming into the windshield, so she could make out the image of the person driving.

Her husband broke her out of her trance like state. He had questions, and they were one right after the other. She pulled her arms down to her side, opened her eyes, and looked at him, annoyance filled her face.

"Sorry Eva, but look at the driver's side of the car," he pointed, stunned.

She followed his gaze, and her eyes went wide at what she was seeing. She moved closer to the door, peering in; the fog was getting less and less dense around them, and a form was taking shape in the driver's seat.

"What thee absolute hell?"

She turned to see Kris right behind her.

"Shhh... I need to concentrate."

"Sorry."

The form was continuing to take shape, and as it did, Eva stood up and took a step back, stepping on her husband's foot and tripping.   He caught her and righted her.

"Oh my God," she said, inaudibly.

"What," he asked, impatiently.

"I know who that is."

The outline she expected to see, was not the one she was seeing. The figure was definitely forming into a female form. She was sure it might be Chrissy, and she'd been all wrong about Gerard, or that maybe they were working together. Eva couldn't even think along those lines, right now.

No, it wasn't Chrissy, thankfully, she thought. The image had longer, darker hair, up in a ponytail. She was wearing dark sunglasses. She was obviously trying to hide her face with them.

Eva had just seen that hair and face though, not even three hours ago.

"How?"

"What," her husband implored.

"It looks like Gemma, our new nail tech. But why?"

"She's new. Why would she be tailing you and trying to scare you?"

"I don't know," she stuttered.

"Do you have your phone," she asked.

"Yeah, why?"

"Try to get a picture of this, if you can. I'm not sure it'll even be possible, but try."

He pointed his phone toward the image and took a picture. He pulled up the picture, and showed her what he was able to get, and they both were slack jawed.

In unison, they both said, "holy shit!"

"Send that to my phone." Eva said in a hurry.

Eva was pacing back and forth so much her husband stepped in to stop her in mid pace.

"Hey! Enough pacing, we need to get out of here, before someone sees my car and calls on the cops to check."

"Oh gosh, you're right. Let me just grab everything, and we can get the hell out of here."

She blew out the candle and the fog disappeared immediately, halting both of them in mid clean up.

"Does that usually happen," he asked.

"Maybe it's just this spell, I'm not sure. It typically fades naturally."

She threw all her paraphernalia into her bag, and they made their way back up to the car. They both jumped in quickly, and Kris took off.

Silence filled the air in the car, and Eva felt the need to break it.

"Now that I've done the spell, and we have the picture, I'm not sure what to do," she lamented.

Kris peered over at her, and picked up her hand, he gave her palm a soft kiss, trying to calm her. He had been thinking about the same thing. It wasn't like they could go to Lt. Murphy with that picture. He would ask how they got it and if they told him the truth, he'd put them both on a 24 hour psych watch.

"I'm not sure how to handle this new information, yet," he admitted.

She didn't expect him to have all the answers for her, but she was glad that he was here with her.

"So, do you think I'm Glenda the Good Witch, or Winifred from Hocus Pocus?" She was trying to lighten the mood.

He chuckled lightly, "I really haven't decided yet, but I don't think either one of those really fits you. I'm thinking more along the lines of Sabrina the Teenage Witch, myself."

She lightly punched his arm, laughing. "Seriously, that's what you came up with?"

"Hey, I'm not acquainted with all the celeb witches, this is all new to me."

"Well, if I'd be anyone, I think I am more like Cassie Nightingale, from "The Good Witch", on the Hallmark Channel."

"Interesting. I may have to go home and check that out," he said, teasing.

"Seriously though, did it really bother you, seeing me in that element? I'm worried that I might have scared you, and you'll never think the same of me, ever again."

He looked thoughtful for a second. "Actually, surprisingly, it really didn't bother me, which kinda scares me. What does that say about me, huh? I digress, deep down, I know you are still the same beautiful, kindhearted woman I fell in love with, twenty-two years ago."

She let out the tiniest sigh of relief. Eva closed her eyes until they reached home. It was only ten, so the kids would surely still be up.

They took her bag of goodies and discarded them in the trash bin in the garage. She had kept one bag in her hand that she had left in the back seat after shopping. That bag had contained a little treat for the kids. She would never hear the end of it, if they hadn't gotten them anything.

Chapter 24

Once she got the kids in bed and shut everything down, she retreated to the respite of her bedroom. Kris lay there reading a car magazine, and looking as if nothing completely weird had happened tonight.

Eva just shook her head in disbelief. "You look all comfy and relaxed," she noticed.

"Don't let the calm fool you, I had some Maker's 46 while you were taming the animals," he grinned.

"Maybe I should try that."

"It would work wonders to calm your nerves, that's for sure."

She climbed into bed, feeling the days events catch up with her as she laid her head on her pillow. She was breathing slowly and calmly, as she tried to get comfortable. It proved more difficult than it should've been.

"Ugh, I can't get comfortable, no matter what I do," she said, exhausted.

"I know what might calm you down; even make you completely forget about what happened today," he winked at her.

Laughing, she just rolled her eyes to the back of her head.

"You always think that's the cure for everything."

"Someday woman, it might be."

She kissed him, and snuggled in closer. He enveloped her in his cocoon of safety. He would always be that for her.

Listening to his easy breathing and the steady beat of his heart, it only took a few minutes before the exhaustion took over, and she fell asleep.

It wasn't a dreamless sleep though.

Chapter 25

The darkness set in, and she was right back where she had grown up, in Connecticut.

Wondering why she was back in the woods near her childhood home, Eva searched. She looked over her shoulder, for anything that would give her an idea of why she was here. It was dark, and sinister, as always.

The wind picked up a bit, and the branches on the trees were whipping side to side. The moon was the only light she had, and it wasn't even full. She noticed that it was more like a waning crescent.

She continued walking, but did full turns, as she did. She wanted to be aware of anything that might come at her. It was then that she noticed a faint light farther into the forest. She knew this area well, she grew up roaming these woods with her sister, many times.

The thought of her sister made her heart ache. She hadn't seen her in a couple years. Pushing that aside, she headed toward the faint light that was beckoning her.

She had walked farther than she thought. She was deeper into the woods. She stared at the reason for the light, she was staring into a small bonfire that was lit in a clearing. No one seemed to be near it though, keep watch on it. She walked closer, all the while keeping her gaze floating around her, looking for trouble.

There was a large log facing the fire, as if people were sitting around it roasting marshmallows, but she knew otherwise. She sat on the big sturdy log, taking in the fire and it's warmth. She let her eyes close for a moment, taking in the heat.

Her eyes flew open when she heard a faint rustling of leaves. She jerked her head up, stood and looked towards the direction the noise came from. She saw a figure coming toward her. She put up a defensive front, waiting for her visitor to make their move.

"Eva please, no need to be defensive dear," the image declared.

Eva thought she was losing her mind. The voice had a familiar sound, but it wouldn't come to her. Then it hit her... It sounded just like her mother Alma, but she was dead, it couldn't be.

"Who's there," she yelled.

"My dear, don't you recognize your own mother's voice? Have I been banned from your thoughts and memories for so long, that you don't even recognize me?'

Eva stepped back many feet away from the incoming figure. She nearly tripped over a tree root, but she'd caught herself.

"My mother is dead, she's been dead almost twenty five years. Try again!"

As the figure inched closer to the bonfire, it became clearer, it did look like Eva's mother, that she was sure of, but how.

Mouth open, she stuttered, "what the hell is going on?"

The figure in front of her was in a flowing white organza gown, her hair was framed around her face, it did look like her mother, but not quite the way she remembered. This woman was younger, beautiful, and looked happy.

"Why am I here? Why are you here?"

Questions flowed from Eva faster than she could get answers.

The figure put her arms out, as if asking her to sit and join her.

"My darling Eva, you've turned into such a beautiful woman, I knew you would."

Eva stood, a statue of stone. Internally, she wanted to run, and she wanted to wake up. She tried hard to make herself wake up from this nightmare.

"That won't help anything, you won't awaken, until I let you," her mother warned.

"What do you want from me, then?"

Motioning her to sit, yet again toward the log, she herself, moved fluidly through the fire, and positioned herself on the log. Eva stared in shock, but moved slower, and more aware, toward the log. She stopped a mere three feet from it. She still was not trusting, and she gave her mother a wary look.

"Eva, I'm not going to hurt you. Sit, please."

Eva did as asked. Still maintaining some distance, she sat at the other end of the seven-foot log.

"It's wonderful to see you Eva." Her mother looked truly happy and emotional.

"I'm sorry, I'm not sure what to say mother, this is all too much for me to take in."

"I understand. I brought you here to talk to you, it was the only way. I see you're practicing again," she merely stated it as fact.

Eva shot her a look of surprise. "How'd you know that?"

Laughing in a high pitch, she wagged her finger toward her daughter, "Oh dear, I see all. I also know that I have grandkids, and that you're married to a lovely man, who loves you very much. I know you manage a salon, which is why you are all of a sudden using your family gift." She said all of this to her, a little too smugly for Eva's liking.

"Okay fine, so you know all about me and my family. It still doesn't explain why I am here with you."

Alma stood, walking around the fire this time. "My child, I know and feel your anxiety. I felt it the first time you decided to open the book. I mean no harm to you, you're my daughter, I love you. I know at the end, I messed up, and I paid dearly for it. I want to make sure you don't make the same mistakes I did."

Air ripped from Eva's lungs. She knew she made mistakes, and it destroyed Eva, her sister, and their dad. Was this her penance, was she trying to get into heaven now?

All these thoughts were running though Eva's head, when she looked up and her mother was mere inches from her.

In a defensive move, Eva jerked back, and fell off the log, hitting her head on the earth floor.

Grabbing the back of her head, expressing some expletives that would make her kids blush, she tried to regain her footing, putting more distance between her and her mother.

Inching closer, Eva's hands came up in a halting position, she didn't want her mother any closer.

"Eva, I swear I'm not going to harm you. Please put your hands down."

She slowly lowered her hands to her side.

"Why did you want to see me mother? You have to see this from my point of view, I'm having a very hard time with this."

With a resigned look in her eyes, she shook her head in acknowledgment.

"I'm sorry if I scared you, that was not my intention. I just wanted to talk to you, and tell you to be very careful what you spell. I don't want anything bad to happen to you, not like what happened to me."

"Okay fine, but you couldn't have thought of a better way to do that?"

"I guess this wasn't the best idea, I get it. I didn't have a lot of time to think about it. You need to know something. Those people you're trying to deal with there, with this investigation; they're not who you think they are."

Eva let that sink in, looked questioningly at her mother, "How do you know about any of this?"

Alma turned away from her daughter, and gazed at the moon.

"I just know, and that's all you need to know," she said, abruptly.

"Well mother, that isn't a good enough reason, you gotta do better than that."

"Why can't you just take my word for it. WIll you listen to me, for once?"

Eva's brows knit together, thinking her mother had to be kidding. After everything she put them through, that she would think she'd just take her word for it? Is she kidding?

So Eva did what she had to do to end this, this nightmare she was having, she agreed to her mother's statements.

"Okay mom, I will be very careful. I think the police will finish the investigation anyway." She hoped that would satisfy her mother.

"Oh please, I wasn't born yesterday, Eva. I know you; you thought you could placate me with that little performance?"

Stunned, Eva walked closer to her mother, and looked her straight in the eyes.

"What do you suggest I do, mother?"

The hatred in her voice took Alma by surprise, but she soon recovered her stance as the dominant, more powerful female.

"You are playing with fire, child. You don't have the wherewithal or the guts to deal with what you started," she glared.

Turning on her mother, Eva was done.

"This just burns my ass, Mom!"

Backing up a fraction, her mother smacked her across her face, making Eva almost fall.

"Don't you talk back, young lady. You have no idea what I could unleash on you."

Thunder rumbled behind her, lightning streaked across the sky. Eva didn't know if it was her mother's doing, or just a coincidence.

Defeated, Eva sat still, holding her cheek. "Fine, what should I do, or not do, in this case?"

"First of all, give your mom a hug. I've missed you so."

Eva got to her feet, feeling deflated. She walked over and gently hugged her mother, or the ghost of her mother, she didn't know what was real anymore.

"Oh darling, my sweet Eva."

The hug seemed to last too long for Eva's taste.

"Mom, could you just please tell me what you think I should do with all that I have found."

"Okay dear, sit. I was thinking about it, and I think you may be better off going straight to that Gemma girl, and ask her a few questions. One in particular... Why was she tailing you? You can show her the image Kris got of her from when you cast that last spell. She could hardly deny it."

"That's not bad Mom. What about uncovering the weapon Gerard has in his mother's box?"

"I'm still deliberating on that one."

Alma looked at her daughter, the love in her eyes was unmistakable, but there was hesitancy there, too.

"Eva, I really didn't mean to frighten you, and I'm sorry I hit you. Are you okay?"

"I'm fine mom, but thanks for apologizing. It seems you still have a bit of that darkness in you, huh?"

With her head down, and ashamed, she nodded toward her daughter in acknowledgment.

"I'm sorry mom; I'm sorry the darkness won't leave you, but just so you know, I see the light in you, it's there. You just need to go to it, okay?"

Tears rolled down her eyes. Eva's mom touched the spot where she had hit her moments ago, and the tears came faster. She knew there was good in her mom, and she hoped she'd feel it, too.

"Love you Mom."

Alma looked sad, but whispered her love to her daughter, then turned around and walked back towards the deep forest.

Eva stood in the clearing for a minute, then headed back to where she started this journey. She prayed she would wake up from this bizarre dream she was in, soon.

Everything suddenly went black, then bright; too bright to be in the woods. Eva squinted into the brightness, and saw her husband looking down at her, a curious and worried expression on his face.

"Man that had to have been some dream you had."

She looked around at her surroundings, and plopped back against her pillow. She lett out a huge sigh of relief. She was back in her own house.

Still staring, Kris raised his eyebrows at her, waiting for some response.

"You wouldn't believe me if I told you." And she bounded for the bathroom, saying nothing else.

Chapter 26

Eva had a bit of a spring in her step. She had a plan of attack, so to speak. She was going to confront Gemma.

She was almost finished getting ready for work, when the phone rang.

She picked it up, and said "Hello?"

It was quiet at first, then came the mutated voice.

"Don't you ever learn? Do you want to end up like poor Trudy? Mmmm... the blood pulling on the stairs in the alley was something to see, it was a little too salty for my taste, but still rather satisfying."

Speechless, Eva choked, dry heaving into the kitchen sink. A laugh vibrated from the other end, pulling her out of her sickness.

"You sick son of a bitch, Gerard! I know it's you. I know you killed Trudy!"

It had all just come out in one fell swoop, and she didn't mean to give any of that away, but she couldn't listen to anymore of his disgusting spewing.

"You know nothing!" And he was gone.

"Crap, Crap and double crap!"

This was not how this was supposed to go down, she thought. She just tipped her hand. She was screaming at herself in her head, and then a thought occurred to her, he doesn't know that she knows about Gemma.

That gave her an idea. She'd need to get Gemma into the shop before anyone else got there. She needed to confront her, and see if she'd talk; before this whole thing goes South.

She checked her cell phone to see if she'd remembered to add her number to her contacts. Her hands were shaking with nervous energy as she scrolled through her contacts.

"Oh thank God I am so anal about being organized. I have her number."

Pushing the call button, she swayed back and forth with every ring. She answered on the fourth.

"Hello?"

"Gemma, it's Eva from the salon. How are you?"

The silence was deafening on the other end. When she finally spoke, surprise and caution coated her voice.

"Eva, I'm fine and you?"

"Just fine, thanks. I was wondering if you'd be able to come into the salon this morning, before we open. There are some papers I still need you to fill out, and I'd like to get that finished, and everything entered into the computer. Do you mind meeting me there?"

Eva bit her lower lip in anticipation.

Gemma finally agreed. "I guess I could come in this morning."

"Great, I'll meet you there in an hour, if that works?"

"Sure, see you then."

Chapter 27

Eva was never one for being superstitious, but she felt the need to do a protection spell.

"Shit! I never wanted to start this whole magic thing, ever again, and now look at me."

She was searching for a black velvet bag that she had kept in an old wooden trunk that she had taken from her parents house in Connecticut. It was the only thing she had wanted from that place. She kept the trunk in the basement, where her kids wouldn't see it.

As she searched through the old dusty trunk, she found it filled with a few things from her past. This is where she had kept the old book of spells that had been handed down to her from her grandmother, whom she adored. It was her father's mother, and she was strictly an Earth witch. She never dabbled in black magic, which is probably why Eva loved her so much.

Remembering Grandma Lilly, she could see her out in her garden, wearing her flowing gray dress that came to her ankles, her beautiful long silver hair pulled into a french braid. She was tall, thin and had hardly any wrinkles on her beautiful alabaster skin, which made Eva wonder if she'd ever done a youth spell on herself.

She remembered gardening with her every spring. Her Grandma Lilly could grow the most beautiful flowers, and the most abundant vegetable and herb garden anyone had ever seen. She would help her grandma every Saturday in the summer. That was when her hometown would have their farmers market.

Her garden was way too much for her grandma and her family to eat, so she would take half of her vegetables, herbs and flower bouquets to the market, to sell.

Eva loved helping her grandma put the flower bouquets together. SHe would wrap them in burlap and tie a colorful raffia ribbon around it. The presentation was simple, but beautiful.

She would always tell Eva what herbs would be good for cooking, and which ones would be good to cast a spell with. The only spells Grandma Lilly ever cast were for people in town that she would hear were having a rough time of it, or those that were ill. Letting out a gentle sigh, Eva continued her search.

"Ah, there it is," she said. She picked up the black velvet bag that had long satin ties wrapped around it.

She opened the bag and tipped it over into her hand, where a black obsidian stone with a black silk string running through it, fell into her hand. Now all she needed was her black candle that she used the other night, three sticks of Dragon's blood incense, which she was looking for, in the trunk, but stopped short when she noticed a small brown box in the bottom corner of the trunk.

Picking it up, she stared at the small unadorned box for a second.

"Hmm, I've never seen this before," she said, holding it up.

She turned the box over in her hand multiple times, before giving into her curiosity and opened it slowly. Her eyes lit up like a kid in a candy store. She stared down into the box, at the most sparkling of all pieces of jewelry she'd ever seen. It was a stunning sapphire ring, in platinum or sterling silver, she wasn't sure, but it was an emerald cut, and at least three carats. Confused, she wondered where this had come from. She didn't remember taking anything that looked like that from the house.

At the bottom of the box, an inscription read, "My Lilly Love."

Holding the ring in her fingers, she wondered if it had been put in her trunk by mistake.

This ring had to have been from her Grandfather, to her Grandma Lilly. Unfortunately Eva's grandpa had passed before Eva was born, so she never got to meet him, but knew he had to have been special, because her grandma had never remarried. He was her one and only true love, as she had reiterated to her a multitude of times growing up.

"Back to the task at hand, Eva," she said out loud to no one.

She put the ring back into the box, and she stowed it back in the trunk where she found it.

She continued searching for some incense, when she finally found what she was looking for.

Not too often does one need Dragon's Blood incense, she thought.

She grabbed three sticks, and the stone necklace, before she closed and locked the trunk back up, and made her way upstairs.

Pulling out a small bunch of sage, a glass bowl and salt, she set out to perform the protection spell. It was merely a precaution, she thought to herself.

Lighting the sage, she walked through the first floor of the house, smudging every nook and cranny.

Lighting the black candle and the incense, she took the black obsidian out of the bag, held it over the flame, and waved it over it a few times, then she started the incantation.

"I consecrate this stone with fire."

She went to the incense, and waved the stone over the smoke, and said, "I consecrate this stone with air."

While standing in front of the glass bowl she had filled with water, she submerged the stone in the water while saying, "I consecrate this stone with water."

She then grabbed the salt and sprinkled it into the bowl where the stone lay. She made sure to get some of the salt onto the stone, and said, "I consecrate this stone with earth."

She picked up the stone from the bowl of water, held it in her right hand against her belly. She closed her eyes and started to visualize the sphere of white light encircling her and as she continued to do this, the sphere of light got stronger as she inhaled, then as she exhaled.

Eva saw a beam of energy shine directly into the stone. She'd always been good at the protection spells, those always seemed to come natural to her.

While her eyes were still closed, she recited, " I imbue this stone with the power to protect me from anyone wishing to do me or my family harm. I imbue this stone with the power to shield me and my family from misfortune. May this stone watch over us and keep us all from danger. So it must be"

Taking a final deep breath, she blew on the stone and knew the spell had been cast.

Knowing that the obsidian looked like a regular necklace with a black stone on it, she put it over her head and wore it as such. The closer the better, she thought.

Before heading out the door to meet Gemma, she blew out the candle, made sure the incense had burned fully, and dumped out the salt water, and put the glass bowl into the dishwasher.

She left the house looking like she hadn't done anything special to it. It especially didn't look like any spells had been cast.

Chapter 28

Eva arrived ten minutes before Gemma was to show up. She checked her phone again, to make sure the photo from the embankment was still there, showing the image of Gemma in the car.

"It's still there, good."

Walking to the front entrance of the shop, her heart started thudding in her chest. She had no real plan on how to bring up the subject so out of the blue, that was going to prove a real challenge. She knew she needed to get a grip.

She was always the first one in every morning, walking into a dark, and a little eerily quiet hundred year old building. It was never Eva's favorite thing to do. She walked straight to the light switches, flipping every single one on, before doing anything else. Today was going to be no different.

She swore there were ghosts in the building. From time to time, the front door that's made of heavy wood and glass, would open on its own. She would always make light of it, by saying it was just their resident ghost.

She stopped what she was doing when she heard the door on the spa side open and close. Eva's throat felt like it would close up, with anxiety. Obviously Gemma had just come in.

Walking from the spa side, she heard her say,"Eva, are you here?"

Eva's voice cracked a bit when she tried to reply, "yeah, I'll be right with you."

She came out of the break room, and saw Gemma heading to the front desk. She headed in that direction; gathering all her strength, and made her mouth tip up into a small smile.

"How are you this morning," she asked, hoping her shaky voice didn't give her away.

Gemma looked up from the chair she was sitting in, and Eva noticed she had a bruise on her temple. It looked as though she had tried to use makeup and the styling of her hair differently to try to cover it up, but it didn't quite work.

Gemma noticed Eva staring, and turned away from her.

"So, what else did I need to fill out," she asked, trying to take the attention off her face.

Eva walked around to the filing cabinet, making it look like she was searching for forms. She was trying to think of a way to break into the questioning, she so badly wanted to start.

Eva pulled out her phone, brought the picture up, but didn't show her right away.

"Gemma, how did you get that bruise on your temple, there?

Immediately Gemma tried to hide it.

"Oh, I hit it on a cabinet when I was cleaning."

"Wow, that must have hurt. Are you sure it wasn't when you were chasing me around town last night?" Eva just blurted it out.

Gemma looked stunned, and tried to up her shocked face, by looking chagrined by her accusation.

"What are you talking about," she asked, innocently.

Eva brought her phone around and showed her the image.

"I thought maybe you hit your head when you were racing around town, right here." She showed her the photo of her in the car.

Gasping for words, Gemma tried to back peddle, but Eva could see by her face, she knew she was done.

"Let me just ask you one question. Why me?"

A myriad of emotions played over her face, before she straightened up, and looked her in the eye.

"You stuck your nose where it didn't belong."

"Excuse me? What do you mean by that?"

Gemma stood, trying to retreat, but Eva wasn't done with her yet. She wanted answers. She blocked her from leaving, but Gemma pushed her aside.

Following her towards the spa, Eva piped up, "I need to know why you would try to run me off the road?"

Spinning on her heel, Gemma got in her face.

"You have no room to talk, you saw me get run off the road and you didn't even stop to help me," she accused.

Not backing down, Eva threw it right back in her face, "You hit my rear bumper, and were chasing after me for miles with your brights in my face, and I want to know why?"

Gemma's face was getting red and angier by the second. Eva could see it, but she was not backing down, she wanted answers.

"You answer me, or you're fired."

Displaying a smile only the devil would love, Gemma leaned in, "Pfft, I wouldn't work here, if this was the last place on earth," she spat out with an odd accent. She threw Eva her key, and walked out the door.

"Well, that didn't exactly go as planned. I guess I need to do a little more digging into Miss Gemma Pomeroy's history. And did she have some kind of accent?"

Eva would have to think on that later. She heard the door to the salon open and close, so she straightened herself up and headed over to the other side.

The girls started shuffling in, one by one. Eva had plans to ask Chrissy where Gemma had worked previously, but Chrissy still hadn't shown up. She was going to have to tell them that Gemma had a change of heart about working here, too. She noticed the schedule, and Chrissy's looked like it had some cancellations this morning, but there were still a few on for this afternoon.

Shannon walked in, all smiles and in an upbeat mood. "Has our delinquent come in yet, this morning," she asked.

Eva couldn't help but chuckle, because that's just how Shannon was.

"She doesn't have any appointments until this afternoon.

"Question for you," Eva said, in a low voice.

"What's that?"

"Did you girls do any kind of background check or work history inquiry on Gemma, before you hired her? I was just looking for her info or resume, but I couldn't find anything. She was in earlier, and she gave me her key back. She decided against working here."

"Oh damn! All we did was have a thirty-minute talk with her, and she told us about all of her experience. I can't remember if we wrote down the places she had previously worked at. We'll have to ask Chrissy. Did she say why she didn't want the position now?"

"Not in so many words. Maybe it just wasn't a good fit," Eva said, cringing inwardly.

Getting more and more antsy by the minute, Eva tried to remain impassive, but was thinking they really didn't have a clue about her at all.

"Had you bothered to call any of her previous workplaces? Or did you guys do a Facebook check on her already?" She tried to sound impartial, and hoped that she was convincing.

169

"I'm sure Chrissy or Sarah would have checked her Facebook or Instagram page. I don't do social media like they do, ya know."

"Yeah, I'm not much into social media myself, but I do have Instagram, because my kids both have it."

"Gemma seemed like a pleasant girl. I liked her," Shannon said.

"Yeah, it's too bad it didn't work out."

It took all Eva had not to open Shannon's eyes to the real Gemma Pomeroy; like, "did you know she has something to do with the murder of Trudy Marshall, and she nearly killed me the other night while she was tailing me home. But no, Eva kept a straight face and just nodded.

Heading to her station to set up for her first client, Shannon was blissfully unaware of the bullet they may have just dodged. Eva was going to have to do some more digging.

In her head, she thought, "I just keep getting myself deeper and deeper into this mess. When is it going to end? And, how is it going to end? And, what does Gemma have to do with it?"

She knew she would have to stay dubiously alert to conversations all around her, yet not give herself away.

All throughout the day, she worked on her listening skills. No one was the wiser, but then again, neither was she. She learned nothing new, so she was going to have to yet again, ask her husband, the computer whiz, for some help on finding out any background information on Gemma.

It was nice to see Chrissy in her element, doing hair, gabbing with the clients, as if nothing was wrong. It was almost as if she wasn't the main suspect in a murder.

To give her clients some credit, they were all so nice, and didn't for once believe that she could have anything to do with killing Trudy.

Eva did overhear a couple of the ladies say, "not like she didn't have it coming. She had a lot of enemies around this town."

Eva knew Trudy wasn't generally liked. She tended to flaunt her wealth and didn't give two cents about anyone but herself. Some of the comments made about Trudy really didn't surprise her all that much, but she couldn't exactly go up to any of the people making them and start asking questions. They'd know she was eavesdropping.

Still, as Eva sat at her desk, she thought, no matter how miserable Trudy was to people, she didn't deserve to die the way she did. She was still a human being.

Lots of talk, but nothing helpful for nine straight hours. The salon was buzzing with chatter, but it was just the normal yammering.

Eva knew someone who might be able to help her with getting information on someone. If Kris couldn't help her, she was facing a possible losing battle. She was far from ready to throw in the proverbial towel on this.

Chapter 29

It was just after 6:30pm, when Eva pulled into their garage. The whole time she drove home, she'd kept an eye on her rear view mirror. She was still a little paranoid and wanted to make sure she wasn't being followed again.

She had never not once felt unsafe in this town, until recently. Still on high alert, she got out of her car and looked out from the driveway, onto the street, searching up and down, for anything that was out of the ordinary. Kids were playing in their yards, parents were coming home from their long days at work, but nothing that struck her as odd. She closed the garage door and headed inside.

First the smell came, then she heard laughing. She proceeded into the kitchen, where she found both kids and Kris huddled near the stove, cooking.

"What is this," she asked, smiling.

Both kids turned and ushered her out of the kitchen in a hurry.

"You can't come in, not until dinner is ready Mom."

Stymied, Eva laughed and tried to push her way back towards the kitchen, but they continued to block her way.

"We'll come get you when it's finished," Kris explained.

"Okay, should I be afraid?"

He took umbrage at her lack of faith in him and gave her a pouty look.

"Really Eva, you're not the only one in this family who knows how to cook, ya know."

Feeling a little bad, she smiled and tried to backtrack and play up the fact that she knows he can cook. He was a really good cook as a matter of fact.

"I'm sorry honey. I thought it was just the kids cooking, not you."

"Uh huh..."

She let him go back to the kitchen, while she headed for their bedroom. She needed to change into more comfy clothes.

Dinner did smell fantastic, and she was looking forward to it. She hadn't gotten a chance to eat lunch earlier.

She heard the call from the kitchen that dinner was indeed being served. She was starving, and really hadn't had much of an appetite lately. Eva was definitely going to indulge in whatever her family so lovingly cooked for her tonight though.

"Mmmm, something smells divine in here." she walked into the kitchen, to see three of her favorite people smiling at her.

"It's your favorite, bake ziti," both kids said.

Smiling wide, and nostrils flaring, taking in the delicious smell, Eva made her way to the kitchen table where they had everything set out and ready to go. The baked ziti, salad and fresh baked bread was displayed like a restaurant.

"Wow, you guys have been busy. This looks delicious."

"C'Mon mom, sit."

"Thanks everyone!"

Looking at her husband, she smiled and gave him a slight wink. She thought she had to be the luckiest girl in the world.

After she and Kris cleaned up the dishes, which both kids skipped out on, Eva curled her arm around her husband's elbow.

"Thank you for dinner, it was amazing."

"Hey, I told you I knew how to cook."

Laughing, she gave him a peck on the lips.

"Thanks for taking my mind off things for a bit."

"Anytime. You know, there are other things we can do that would totally make you forget what day it is. He looked at her while giving her that sly smile she loved.

Shaking her head, with a slight smile, she said "I've got a favor to ask."

Her voice took on a more serious note.

"Okay, what is it," he asked with caution in his eyes.

"I need your help to do a background check on Gemma. The girls said they never asked her for references, or any real work history. They may have looked at her Facebook page, but that's it. There is something about her, I don't like. I don't trust her."

"Did you confront her about the other night and her following you home?"

"I did confront her. She had a nasty bruise on her temple, which I assumed she got from going down the embankment, but her reply was less than forthcoming. She told me to stop sticking my nose in everything, basically, and she quit."

"You do have a way with people, don't you?" He was only half laughing.

She gave him a light punch to the bicep. "Ow!" He grabbed his arm and gave her his best fake cry.

"She got very defensive with me, so she obviously has something to hide and I want to know what it is. She is connected to this murder somehow. Oh, come on, will you please help me? You have a way with computers that I don't."

"Well, I should, it is my job after all. Okay, let's go to the office, and we'll see what we can dig up."

"Thank you!"

She jumped up off the couch and grabbed his hand, pulling him up. SHe wanted to get started right away.

Kris' office was not quite the same as Eva's was. Hers was simple, a desk, chair, laptop, tons of books on a cherry wood bookshelf that lined a whole wall, along with some paintings, mostly from the kids, and her favorite black and white buffalo check wing back chair in the one corner.

Kris' was full of electronic equipment; a desktop computer, with three large flat monitors on an L shaped desk, and a laptop. His black leather couch did take up one wall, a basic walnut bookshelf on another wall, full of computer books, but the electronics overshadowed everything else. He did a lot of his work from home, so he needed all the necessary equipment.

Eva pulled her desk chair from her office and put it next to his chair, and watched him start everything up.

Waiting was not one of her strong suits, and she was getting antsy. Her knee started bouncing up and down.

Kris put his hand on it and pushed it down.

"Nervous much?"

"Ugh, sorry I just want to find something I can use."

"I get it, but you realize some things that I may have to do, may not exactly be legal, right?"

"I know. It's not like I'll be able to take any of it to the police anyway. I just want to see what her address and work history is. Maybe you can see if anything comes up under a criminal background check, as well. I guess, let's just see how much you can find first, then we'll go from there."

She watched him type so much stuff into a search engine, and all she gave him was her first and last name.

How can he be typing so much? She didn't understand any of it, but that's why she went to the expert.

After lots of typing, he drew his brows together, "I don't get it."

"What? What did you find?"

"Not a damn thing. It's like she doesn't even exist. Are you sure this is her name? Gemma Pomeroy?"

"Yes, I checked the contract that she signed. Try it with her middle initial, J. I forgot about that."

He added the J into the search.

"I tried all sorts of variables, and I even put her through AFIS, and a couple of FBI's finest sites, and nothing. I've got one more place I can try; the dark web. Not someplace anyone should ever try to go to."

"What in heaven's name is the dark web?"

"That would be the underbelly of society, dear. We can see if anyone sold this name to someone recently. People's identities get bought and sold all day long there. That's how identity theft occurs most of the time."

"Wow, how do I not know this," she asked, completely taken back.

"It's not something that is advertised."

He continued typing from one search engine to another, when he finally stopped and started reading something to himself.

"Did you find something?"

"Maybe. It looks as though someone bought or shall I say created, a new identity in the name of Gemma J.Pomeroy, about a month ago."

"Does it say who bought or created it?"

"No. That info will take a little more skill to find out. Give me a minute, and we'll see what I can find."

Eva hated sitting around not doing anything, but she didn't want to leave the office, in case Kris found something. She gnawed on her lower lip, her knee bouncing to the rhythm of her pulse, and she looked like she was waiting for a pregnancy test to finish processing. She did that when she got nervous.

Kris pulled her out of her nervous trance, "hey, do you know anyone named Jack W?"

"No, not right off hand, why?"

"That's the only name I am finding, for a possible buyer of the identity."

"Jack, Jack, Jack W...." She said the name over and over, out loud, hoping it would conjure a memory. She stopped when it hit her. The only Jack she knew, was Emma's ex-husband. Jack Walker.

"Nah, can't be him," she said.

"Who are you talking about?"

"What?"

"Can't be who? You said, it can't be him."

She hadn't even realized she said that out loud.

"Oh, the only Jack W I know, is Emma's ex-husband."

"Hmm..."

"What's that supposed to mean, hmm?"

"I was just saying, hmm."

"You think it could be Emma's ex?"

"I don't know what to think anymore, honestly."

Eva sat back, and tried to relax her uptight shoulders and breathe. She didn't know what to do next. There were no new leads really, just a name of Jack W that bought the identity of Gemma J Pomeroy.

Gemma J, she thought, could be J for Jack. She mused to herself, are they one in same, but how? So many questions, so few real answers.

Eva made up her mind, tomorrow at work she'd ask Emma a few questions about Jack.

Looking at her husband, who was still staring at the computer screen, she announced, "I'm going to talk to Emma tomorrow. I want to see if Jack still lives in town."

Eyeing her suspiciously, he warned, "don't be obvious Eva."

"I won't. I'll be nonchalant." She sat there with a cheshire grin on her face..

Shaking his head, he knew full well, she was going to go head first into the fire, as always.

"Okay honey."

Chapter 30

Thankful for the uneventful morning, Eva headed into work. She had a plan, but no execution on how to start up the conversation and questioning, yet. Her main goal was to not seem obvious. Lately, she wasn't sure she knew how to be, as she told her husband, "nonchalant", about anything.

She arrived at the salon forty minutes earlier than everyone else, because that was her routine. She could get everything set up, and get voicemail messages before everyone got in.

If there were cancellations, she could let the stylist know ahead of time.

She checked the day's schedule, and it looked like Emma would be one of the first ones in.

She thought to herself, this may bode well for a short Q and A. She sat smiling, and waiting.

After she had checked the voicemail, she was thankful there were no new threatening messages on the salon's voicemail. That made Eva breathe a slight sigh of relief.

"Good morning, Eva," Emma said, as she strolled into the salon.

"Emma, good morning. You're here early," she said, a little too excitedly.

"Yeah, the kids are at their Dad's, and I was up early, so I thought, what the hell."

Eva could barely hide her happiness. The fact that she had mentioned her kids being at their dad's, was almost like an invitation to start questioning her. She couldn't help it.

"Oh nice. So Jack is still in the kids lives, regularly?"

"Sure, he has them every week, at some point."

"That must give you a nice break, huh?"

"Usually yes, but the kids always seem to call me for some reason or another." She laughed.

Eva couldn't help herself. "So Jack still lives in Delaware then?"

Crap Eva, can you be any more obvious? She chided herself in her head.

Without even thinking about it, Emma answered her, like nothing was peculiar about her line of questioning.

"Jack has a house on the East side of town, so he's not that far away, unfortunately."

Did she mean to say that last part? Eva tried ignoring that last word, and continued.

"I know you're dating, but does Jack have a special someone, as well?"

Oh dear God, she's going to think I'm interested. Stupid Eva, stupid.

"Don't know, don't care. The less I know about his private life, the better."

Eva wasn't sure what that meant, but it was apparent there was no love lost there. She didn't know what else to ask after that, so she ended the conversation.

She now knows a few things about Jack after the brief talk with Emma, but she will have to research some address info on him, when she gets a free minute.

While Eva was in her own little world, she didn't even hear others entering the salon, until Chrissy came in and plopped a large coffee on her desk.

"Morning sweetheart. I gotcha a coffee from Ciao. Your favorite, hylander grogg, with cream and splenda, right?"

She was quickly brought out of her thoughts. Eva perked up at the smell of the delicious nectar of the caffeine gods that was positioned right in front of her.

She took the top off, and put her nose close to the wafting smell of coffee. She smiled and looked at Chrissy. "Thank you. There is a God."

"Oh honey, you're looking at that coffee like it's Christian Grey sitting on a platter."

She nearly spat coffee across her desk. Eva laughed, and slowly put the top back on. She gently took a small sip of her coffee. She closed her eyes and smiled.

"Sorry, I didn't realize how badly I needed the caffeine fix."

The morning was rather busy, which was a nice change of pace. No one had time to dwell on the recent events that had taken place lately.

By afternoon, the traffic in and out of the shop had slowed down. She was thinking about doing some snooping. Eva did a quick search on her computer, for Jack Walker.

She looked up every now and then, to make sure Emma wasn't near, or anyone else was looking over her shoulder.

She continued looking at everything that her search brought up. He had a Facebook page, there were a few addresses, but she didn't know which one was current, so she wrote down all the ones listed. He even had a MySpace account, as well.

"MySpace? How old is that account?"

Quickly getting out of her search, Eva saw Shannon coming towards her desk, with a question on her face.

"Hey, have there been any other suspects that the police are looking at in Trudy's murder? Anything new you've heard?"

"Not that I'm aware of, why?"

"I was just wondering. I mean, seriously, that woman had more enemies than Hitler. There have got to be more people to look at, than just Chrissy."

Eva looked at Shannon with realization clicking in.

"You think someone is pointing the police in Chrissy's direction, don't you?"

"It's just a little odd, don't you think?"

"Yes, but I know she didn't do this."

"I know, you've been adamant about that for a few days now."

If she only knew why.

"I may call Jerry, to see if he's heard of anyone else they're looking at."

"That's a good idea. Let me know what you find out."

Shannon shook her head, and headed back toward her station grabbing her cell phone. She went to the back of the shop to call Jerry.

The rest of the afternoon, all the way into the evening went by without any drama, which is just the way they all liked it.

Shannon texted Eva later that afternoon.

"Jerry is clueless. He hasn't heard of any new suspects, but I think I may have put a bug in his ear, and he agrees, there is something fishy there. He's going to check it out."

Eva texted her a thumbs up emoji.

Thinking to herself, she admitted that she was happy to have someone else besides her, looking into this more. And with some of his contacts, he may have a better chance at getting more answers, than she would.

Eva closed up her computer, and gathered her stuff from under the desk. She was getting ready to leave for the evening, when Chrissy stopped at her desk.

"Are you leaving soon?"

"Yeah, did you need something before I go?"

"No. I was just wondering if you'd done any other snooping, that you aren't telling me about?"

Well, that came out of nowhere. And just like her husband, she could tell, by her face, that she was hiding stuff from her.

"Okay fine, I've done some other things that I haven't told you about."

"Like what," she pressed.

"I don't want to go into here. If you want, you can stop by my house later this evening, if you think you can leave your house. I'll let you in on everything I've found out, so far."

"Thanks, I want to know everything. I don't want you hiding or embellishing any of it, because you think it might be for my own good."

"Deal."

"Good. I'll be over around 8pm or so, if that works for you."

"That's fine. I'll have a bottle of wine chilled and ready. You're gonna need it."

"Shit!"

Chapter 31

Eva arrived home, to find both kids and Kris hanging out in front of the TV. They were entranced in an episode of Ghost Adventures.

"Hey guys."

"Hey Mom," her oldest piped up. None of them even looked her way.

"Anyone want to help me make dinner?"

No answer. Must be a good show.

She turned and headed for the kitchen. She realized no one cared what they were going to eat tonight.

She looked through the pantry for some sustenance. She felt the air around her shift, and looked over her shoulder to see Kris looking at her, smiling.

"Find anything good?"

"Not yet. Just to give you a heads up, Chrissy will be coming over later. She wants me to fill her in on the calamity that had ensued over the last couple days."

"Oh boy..."

"Yeah, she won't stop asking, until I tell her, and it does kind of concern her, so I'm just going to give her the abridged version."

Kris laughed out loud as he wrapped his arms around her waist and kissed her cheek

"There is no abridged version."

Eva rolled her eyes at him, and walked out of the pantry. She went to the fridge, still searching for something to make for dinner, that didn't include mac and cheese.

She had found some veggies to go with the chicken she took out of the freezer, and she turned to Kris.

"I talked with Emma earlier."

He inclined his head toward her, for her to continue.

"Well, Jack does live in town, still. I'm not sure he is seeing anyone. She didn't seem to care though. From what I gather, there may have been extenuating circumstances to that divorce that none of us know about."

"How so?"

"To quote her, "don't know, don't care" was her attitude toward Jack and his personal life."

"Oh, so maybe there was more to the divorce than just the two of them not getting along anymore, huh?"

"Obviously, but I didn't want to ask anymore questions. I did, however, look online to see where he lived. Four possible addresses popped up. I'll check Emma's address, and I can eliminate that one. The others, I'll have to do drive-by's and see if I get lucky."

"Excuse me, drive-by's?"

"I'm just going to check the addresses and see if I see him outside, or recognize his car. Maybe on the off chance, I will see the girls outside playing, or something, too."

Kris shook his head, not totally convinced her plan would work. He had a feeling that he would lose whatever argument he would start, so kept his mouth shut.

They got through dinner without any major incidents, except the typical whining from the children about not wanting to eat their vegetables.

Eva had just finished cleaning up the kitchen when her cell phone rang. She jerked up, the anxiety pouring through her, and she picked up the phone, looked at the number; and of course it wasn't a number she recognized, but she answered it anyway.

Without even saying hello, the person on the other end started their assault.

"Your children are adorable, Eva. It would be a shame for anything to happen to them, now wouldn't it?"

Eva stood in shock, her voice wouldn't work, her limbs wouldn't move.

"Did you hear me Eva? You better acknowledge me, or else."

Her voice cracked. "I heard you."

"Good, now give up trying to help Chrissy, if you know what's good for your family."

The mere mention of her family had Eva quickly coming out of her shock.

"I know who you are, Gerard and I believe you've brought in help. I will find out who, mark my words, you will go down. You don't scare me. I know you use burner cell phones, so it's pointless for me to tell the police anymore."

She was vibrating with anger and wanted him to know that she wouldn't be bullied.

"You've just sealed your fate, and everyone around you, too."

"Don't you dare threaten me. You have no idea who you're dealing with."

She knew she was challenging the man, even egging him on a little, but she couldn't stop herself.

"Oh dear, I know more than you think I know. I wouldn't get too cocky, if I were you." Click

Her hands were still shaking, and she was breathing heavy. Eva choked back the tears that were burning her eyes, she turned around and ran right into Kris. His anger was radiating off of him.

"Who were you just talking to?"

She hiked her chin up, finding very little bravado in the movement, and told him.

"Jesus Eva, you've got to stop now. The threat is spreading to our children. I'm putting my foot down on this, now."

"I can't stop, not yet. I'm not going to let anything happen to any of you, I swear. Our house is protected."

"Okay, so what happens when the kids go to school, or I go to work; are those places protected, too?"

Seeing his point, but not willing to give in, she took his hands in hers.

"Please trust me. I will make sure this ends, soon."

"How?"

Damn, he wanted a detailed plan. She was at a loss for what to say, she looked him in the eyes, willing him to understand, to see that she could do this.

He pulled her into him tightly, talking into her hair.

"When was Chrissy coming over tonight?"

She pulled back quickly to look at him, and balked.

"Shit, I forgot she was coming. She'll be here soon. I have to get it together."

She kissed him quickly, and walked away, wiping her eyes. She went to their bedroom to change her clothes.

In her closet, she grabbed the most comfortable clothes she could find, threw them on her bed, and went to the bathroom to wash her face, getting rid of any signs that she'd been crying. The last thing Chrissy needed was for her to be an emotional liability.

She looked in the mirror, and shook her head, clearing her mind of the phone call. She put her hair in a quick ponytail, and headed for the stairs, just as the doorbell rang. Eva pasted a smile on her face, and opened the door.

"Chrissy! Come on in."

She walked past Eva, with an air of lightness about her that she hadn't seen earlier. She was counting on Eva to get her cleared of a murder charge.

No pressure there.

Chapter 32

She grabbed the bottle of Chardonnay from the fridge, along with two glasses, and she joined Chrissy in the den.

"Now you're talking," she said.

She took one of the glasses from Eva's hand.

"Yeah, you might need a few, after I explain everything that's happened over the last couple days."

"Damn."

Sitting on the one end of the couch, facing her friend and boss, Eva went into detail, everything that had transpired. Everything from Gemma following her, to the spell she cast to find out, it was indeed Gemma. And to her questioning Emma of Jack's whereabouts. Eva left out the part about the phone call from earlier. She thought Chrissy had enough to worry about.

"Whoa, what? How is Jack involved in all this?"

"Well, once we went to do a background check on Gemma and found zilch, Kris did his thing, and found an identity for Gemma J. Pomeroy, and it had been purchased on the dark web by one Jack Walker. I'm just not sure how he ties in with this. I pulled addresses for Jack off the internet, and I was going to drive by all of them and see what I can find."

"Let's go now."

"Wait Chrissy, you can't go, the police are probably out there somewhere on my street right now, waiting for you to leave, so they can see where you go next."

"You watch too many crime shows. I think I would have noticed if anyone was following me."

"That may be, but I still don't think you should do anything that will draw any more attention to you, than you already have. I'll take Kris with me, okay?"

"This really sucks. You guys get to do all the cool stuff, and I just have to sit here like a grounded teenager."

Chrissy hadn't stayed much longer after their conversation, so Eva went to the kitchen to put the wine glasses in the dishwasher, and the rest of the wine back into the fridge.

Kris sauntered in, with a smug look on his face.

"So when are we going to go address hunting?"

Eva looked at him, confused.

"Do what?"

"I heard you tell Chrissy, that you were going to take me with you, to look at all the addresses you pulled on Jack."

Shit, he overheard me.

"Oh well, I was just trying to placate her, so she wouldn't push the issue of going with me."

"Well, now you can placate me, and let me go with you." He stood with his hands shoved in his pockets, smiling.

Double shit!

Already knowing she wasn't going to win, she accepted the fact that she was going to have a partner in this little adventure.

Eva wasn't sure what side of the law she was on anymore. She'd done spells to find out things, had her husband hack into computers to find information, now she was going to stalk someone.

"It was for the greater good, right?" She figured that had to stand for something.

"You look like you're arguing with your inner self over there. Are you trying to come up with some excuse for me not to go with you?"

Great, now he's psychic.

"No, I'm just deciding when the best time for us to go would be."

Chuckling to himself, he moved closer to her, and whispered in her ear, "you're such a bad actress."

"If you must know, I'm stalling. My nerves are shot and I'm not sure I can do this. I don't know how detectives do this stuff every day. For god sakes, I know who did it, but I can't prove it, the normal way anyway. And then there's this thing with Gemma and Jack. Where the hell do they fit into the scenario? It's all getting overwhelming. On top of all that, I blurted out that I knew it was Gerard on the phone, and that I knew he was the one that killed Trudy."

Kris' whole body stiffened, his jaw was working hard against the strain that was forming in his whole body. His wife had made a huge mistake.

"You did what? You let him know that you knew he killed Trudy? What the hell were you thinking Eva?" His voice raising with each word coming out. "We're as good as dead."

"I'm sorry! He was being such a bully, and threatening our children. I lost it."

Tears welled up in her eyes, but she forced herself to stop. She was stronger than this, and she'd seen far worse.

"What would you have done, if it were you," she challenged.

His face went from angry to thoughtful.

"I guess probably the same thing. That doesn't mean you didn't do anything wrong, though."

"I get that, and I'll take full responsibility, but I need to know you're with me. We need to be a team, now more than ever. To protect our family and ourselves."

He pulled her in closer, holding her tight. It was killing him to see what this was doing to her.

"I'm with you. Now, when are we going on our next adventure."

She felt his smile and looked at him through her tears. She was thankful that she had such an amazing partner in life.

"I can call Jessie to see if she's available to come over and keep and eye on the kids, if you want to take a drive now."

He kissed the top of her head, and let go of the hold he had on her. "That sounds like a plan."

Chapter 33

With the kids being entertained by Jessie. Eva and Kris were on their way to check out the first address she had pulled up earlier.

"Okay, the first place we're heading to is near Alum Creek State park, so just take Old State Rd."

They headed east, and Eva kept looking in her side mirror, just to be on the safe side. She'd become more and more paranoid as the days went on.

"We're not being followed, just so you know."

She shot him a look. "How did you know I was looking for a tail?"

"I pay attention to what you do, and besides, I've been watching my rear view mirror since we left the house."

Half laughing, her tension eased up just a little.

"Well, I am a bit high-strung lately."

"With good reason, but you said our house is protected earlier, what did you mean by that?" He looked truly curious.

She wasn't surprised by his question. She waved her hand in the air, "I put a protection spell on the house yesterday."

He absorbed that new information, but he shook it off.

"I should be surprised by that, but lately, nothing shocks me anymore."

They rode in companionable silence for the rest of the way, until they turned onto Old State Rd.

"It should be down past the campground, on the right. It looks like a subdivision, from what I saw on google maps. A pretty small one."

"Okay, it's right up here on the right, Courtland Dr., and it should be the fifth house on the left."

They turned into the housing development, and she thought it looked newer. It had black Heritage lamp posts set every fifty feet or so. The homes were traditional single family homes. There were brick Tudors, but others looked more colonial. This was not at all what Eva pictured Jack living in.

"The address 776 Courtland. It's right up here, slow down."

"I don't see anyone outside. Do you know what kind of car he drives? That would be helpful."

"All I remember is him having a bigger truck, but he could have gotten rid of that by now."

"There are no lights on in the house, obviously no one is home."

Looking gobsmacked, Eva retorted, "really Sherlock? You got that from no lights being on?"

"Don't get snarky with me. You don't even know what kind of car we're looking for."

Annoyance was rearing its ugly head. This address proved to be crap, so they started to speed up a little, but that's when Eva noticed a car behind them had their turn signal on. They were turning into that driveway.

"Go around the block, and pass that house again, someone just pulled into the driveway."

Kris turned at the next block. He drove around one more time to see if they could get a look at the owner of the house they had just been looking at.

"Crap! That guy has two small children with him. Emma's girls are older than that, and Jack is about four inches taller."

"One address down, two to go. Where is the next address?" Kris was settling into his role as taxi driver.

"We need to head back towards town. The next address is behind the big shopping plaza across from our neighborhood."

"That's where all those new one story apartment homes are; are you sure it's back here?"

Eva double checked her google maps, and nodded.

"Yep, this is the area. At least they're all one story and they have their own driveways. It won't be too hard to see."

"Okay, just tell me when to slow down."

"You're going to want to turn right at Pin Oak Place. It's this first street we'll come to. The address should be the fourth one down, from what I can tell."

He slowed his pace, and Kris was counting four places down in his head, and noticed someone on the front porch.

"Hey, is that Jack there on the porch? I don't know what he looks like."

Eva squinted into the dark, trying to make out the figure on the porch, she was thankful for the light shining from the street lamp, but that was definitely not Jack. Jack is a little taller and a lot skinnier than the gentleman hanging out on the front porch here.

"Nope, that's not him. Okay, I guess we head to the last one. Third times a charm, right?" She looked at Kris, shrugging.

"We'll see. This isn't as much fun as I thought it would be."

"What were you expecting, a lot of James Bond spy stuff?"

"No, but something more entertaining maybe."

She shook her head, laughing. Her husband's idea of fun was not the same as hers.

"This last one is off of Kilbourne Rd. We make a left onto Harris Rd, near the railroad tracks."

"Roger that."

"You're enjoying this a little too much, don't you think?"

"Just trying to keep it light darlin."

Snickering, she half heartedly punched his arm.

They were out in the country, and away from town now. The houses were few and far between out here.

"How far out are we going?"

She was keeping an eye on her google map. "It should be right up here on the left, I think."

He started to slow his speed, not wanting to miss it. "Let me know when."

Eva saw a smaller house coming up on the left, it sat farther back than the others, so it was going to be harder to see anything. There was a bigger truck and a smaller, albeit expensive looking sedan in the drive. The truck still had its headlights on, so they were either leaving, or just getting back.

"Go slower, this is it right here!" She yelled, a little too loud.

Kris slammed on the brakes a little hard, and the car made a high pitched screech sound.

"Jesus Eva, don't yell. I don't want us to attract any attention here."

"Sorry, I just saw the truck with its headlights on and wanted to see if I could make who anyone is."

They weren't able to get a good look, so they kept driving about a half mile, then made an U turn in the middle of the road and Kris headed back to the house.

"Go very slow, so I can see if anyone is out there."

Kris drove a little ways, then he pulled to the side of the road and cut the engine.

"What are you doing?" Eva felt the panic in her.

"We're getting out and going on foot. If I continue to drive by, it'll be more suspicious, especially if someone is outside."

He stepped out of the car, and started walking down the edge of the dirt road. Eva quickly unbuckled herself, got out of the car, and slowly and as quietly as possible, shut her door. She made her way to her husband, but not before she tripped over a rock. She got herself back up and jogged towards him,

"Wait up!"

"Be quiet, we're not trying to announce our visit here."

Her breathing was coming faster, as was her pulse. She didn't think she was cut out for this snooping crap.

"What exactly are we going to do, when we get there?

"Well, I hadn't thought that far ahead. I thought maybe you had an idea," he looked back at her, smiling.

"Are you kidding me!"

"Shhh..."

She then whispered, "are you kidding?"

"The way I see it, it's so dark out here, we can hide behind trees and bushes until we get close enough to see something."

James Bond he wasn't, but god loved him, he was trying to help her out.

As they got closer to the house in question, Eva grabbed Kris' sleeve.

"Wait, what do we do if we see him?"

He rolled his eyes heavenward, he turned and grabbed her arms, willing her to stop the freak out that was coming. In a hushed voice he said, "we'll try to get a picture of him with our phone and the address on the mailbox, okay. That's as far as I've thought. Not sure how helpful that will be, but it's all I've got, right now."

"Oyy..." That was all she could say.

They were standing behind a large maple tree that stood a good fifty feet high and the trunk was at least three feet in wide, wide enough to conceal them.

"I hear voices over by the truck," he said.

"Can you hear what they're saying?"

"No, nothing discernable."

Eva moved in closer and ducked behind a large burning bush.

"What are you doing?" Kris whispered loud enough for her to hear.

She ignored him, and was fishing for her phone.

SHe was hoping she could get a couple pictures. From what she was able to see, she caught a glimpse of Jack, so they were at the correct address, but there were two other people by the truck, as well. One was definitely a woman, by the voice, and not a happy one at that.

"She knew it was me in that car. She had a picture for cripes sake. How she got it, I don't know." The female seemed to be getting upset, talking to the guys.

"How the hell did she get a picture of you in the car, at night?"

Eva recognized the man now yelling at the woman, as Gerard.

"I don't know, but she did. What are you two going to do now?   She obviously isn't scared of you or your vague threats. Maybe you aren't the diabolical mastermind you thought you were."

Eva listened to the conversation as closely as she could, the voice of the woman wasn't one she recognized. She had an accent, but from where, she couldn't place.

She inched closer, moving the branches of the bush apart and putting her phone on camera mode. She was set to take pictures. When she looked at the screen, she shrunk back a little.

"Gemma and Gerard are here, with Jack. What the hell?"

Kris had noticed Eva's flinched reaction to something, and he moved to the bush she was hiding behind.

"What's wrong? Did you see Jack?"

Her voice was shaky, but was still able to get out, "and Gemma and Gerard."

"Seriously?"

She nodded acknowledgment and pointed her phone camera through the bush once again, determined to get the threesome on camera. Her hand shook, and it took all her strength to stop it.

She zoomed in as far as she could without the picture becoming blurry, and snapped a couple shots of the three standing in the driveway.

Kris pulled her back a little and put his ear toward the direction the three stood. He strained to hear anything that they were saying.

"I think I may have to show her just how evil a person can be. She's the one who found Trudy, how could she not think I'm a sick son of bitch," Gerard exclaimed.

"I don't care what you two do, I don't want any of this traced back to me. I brought Gemma into this country for you, got her a fake ID, and she was able to get her way into the salon, so that you had a key to get in. That's the extent that I am helping you, Gerard."

"Listen Jack, you of all people know what that Trudy was capable of, she ruined your marriage. You have every reason for wanting her dead, as anyone else. If this comes back to bite me, you're going down with me."

"The hell I am. I didn't scalp the poor lady, you did."

"Both of you shut up! What are we going to do about the salon manager, she's nosy, and I am not going to be deported back to the Ukraine." Gemma shrieked.

Gerard pulled her to him, and into her ear, ever so lightly whispered, "don't worry my love, no one will send you back. You're here with me, now."

He kissed her hard, and dispassionately. She looked up at him through her lashes, "thank you brother."

Jack piped up, "that's all good and dandy, but how are you going to take care of Eva and Chrissy. I am not involving myself in it.   Emma would kill me, and I'd never see my girls again."

"Well then, you should have thought about that before you went to Vegas with the guys and partied with all bi- sexual men, huh?   Don't worry about the two girls, I'll take care of them, in some form or another.   This Eva is starting to annoy me. I may have to have a little fun with her, before, well, you know."

"Brother, you can't kill her, you need her.   Her vessel anyway."

"I don't want to know, Gerard.   You do whatever you have to.   Now, if you don't mind, I'd like you both to leave." Jack walked away from them, and went into his house.

Eva and Kris looked at each other, dumbfounded, having heard every word of their conversation.

"What in Sam hell," Kris said.   Anger and rage was palpable in his low voice.

Eva motioned for them to get out of the bush.   They stayed low and quiet, walking their way back to their car.

Silence filled the car like a heavy fog.   Eva was petrified at what she heard, and how he was intent on hurting her, before using her.   Using her for what, she still wasn't sure.   She kept it locked up deep inside, for now. She knew Kris was stewing over everything they'd said about her and Chrissy, and didn't want to make things worse.

They were just about to enter their subdivision, when he broke the silence.

"You can't dig anymore into this, I won't let you. I should never have let you go ahead with those spells. Against my better judgement, I let you, and now look at what it's come to."

Brimming with anger, Eva looked over at him, with piercing green eyes.

"You let me? Excuse me, but I have a mind of my own and you are not my boss."

Silence loomed once again. They pulled into their garage. Eva yanked open her car door before Kris had even put it in park, and slammed it hard before she headed inside.

She was ready to scream. She entered the living room where her kids were sitting on the floor. Jessie was behind them on the couch watching them. They were all playing video games. Seeing her kids laughing and safe, Eva's dark mood lightened slightly.

Eva heard the garage door shut, and knew she was going to have to talk to Kris sooner or later, but she wasn't ready yet.

"Hey guys, how was your night," she asked the kids.

"Jessie beat us at monopoly, so she said we could play a game on the PS4."

"Thanks for staying with the kids, Jessie."

"Oh gosh, my pleasure. They weren't any trouble, really."

"It must be the parent complex, then." Eva half laughed, because she knew it was true.

She walked Jessie to the door, paid her and watched her get to her house safely, before she turned to come back in.

"Okay, video game time is up. You both need to get to bed. You have school tomorrow."

In unison, they both groaned. "You don't have to rub it in, Mom."

Both kids stumbled their way upstairs, grumbling the whole way.

"Brush your teeth, to!"

"We know!"

Chapter 34

The silence in the house hung there, like a storm cloud, just waiting for the lightning bolt to hit. Eva was busying herself by cleaning up the kitchen and the kids toys. She noticed that Kris was sitting in his favorite chair, and drinking some of his Makers 46. That was his go to drink, when the shit hit the fan.

Eva knew in her heart that Kris didn't mean what he said. She knew it was more out of fear for her, than anything. He didn't know what to do to fix this. He is the family fixer. Anything breaks, he fixes it. Unfortunately, this wasn't a broken washer, or a kid with a fever. This was much worse, this could be life or death. Her life or death.

She walked into the living room where he sat, and took her seat, right next to him. She reached for his hand, and she was thankful he accepted it.

"I'm sorry. I didn't mean to make you think I was the boss of you."

Eva choked up a little looking at him. "I know, and I'm sorry I stormed out of the car."

"Eva, I'm scared to death for you, and I don't know how to fix it."

Emotions were bubbling up inside her, and she tried to speak, but nothing would come out.

She cleared her throat, hoping that would help, and finally found her voice.

"I'm terrified Kris. I thought I was doing something good by trying to help Chrissy, but now, I could be next. I don't know what to do. We can't go to the police, because I don't have the evidence yet, and I didn't think to videotape any of the conversation we heard tonight. Why didn't I think to do that? I'm so dumb." She leaned forward putting her head in her hands.

Kris lifted her hand for her to get up, and he pulled her into his lap, cradling her. She sat there sobbing, all the emotions from the last few days had finally caught up to her. He said nothing, and just held her tight, rocking her.

A few minutes after she'd stopped crying and her breathing was getting back to normal, Kris said, "can I ask you something?"

Through the hiccups, and sniffling, she shook her head signalling him to ask her what he wanted.

"Are you going to stop looking into this murder now?"

She knew that's what he would ask her, but she didn't have the answer.

"I don't know," was all she said.

Pursing his lips slightly, he didn't respond right away. It took a good minute for him to finally speak up.

"What else can you possibly do? Put yourself in a spotlight for them to come and take you away, and hurt you?"

He immediately regretted saying that, because he now knew what she planned to do. She was going to put herself in the spotlight, so they would take the bait, which was her. She'd then hope someone would catch them.

"No! No, no, no, no."

"What?" She looked startled.

"I know what your plan is, and no you will not use yourself as bait, to get them to come out."

Damn it, he knows me like a frigging book.

"It may be the only way Kris. If they did take me, couldn't you find some sort of tracking device you could put on me, and then notify Lt. Murphy of the situation? We could catch them in the act, so to speak. Isn't there any way we can get some type of device that would track me and a wire where you could hear what they were all saying?

She was excited about this new idea, she was sure it would work.

"I don't like it. For all we know, this Gerard would just sooner kill you first, before doing anything else. There's got to be a better plan." He was trying to steer her away from her hair brained scheme.

"It's perfect, admit it."

"No, I won't admit anything, I don't like it Eva."

Her plan was starting to take shape in her mind, she would need Kris onboard with it though.

He was the tech guy, and she needed to not only have a tracking device on her body somewhere, but also a wire, so any evidence or confession would be recorded.

Eva had gone to bed feeling a bit more positive about everything, because she had a plan, and she knew it would work.

Kris couldn't sleep, his brain was all over the place. He was nervous, scared, and he knew he wouldn't be able to stop her from trying this insane scheme of hers.

He sat staring at his computer, he had just messaged one of his friends that worked at one of those three letter government agencies. He asked him a few questions on tracking devices and wires. His friend didn't even ask why he was interested in such things, he messaged him that he would send him a couple items via private courier and he'd have them tomorrow morning.

"Sometimes it's good to have friends in different places, but god help me if anything bad happens to her," he said to himself.

He sat there for a good hour, staring off into space.

Eva had gotten worried when she rolled over in bed, and he wasn't there, so she had set out to find him. She had an inkling of where he might be, so she went to his office. Sure enough, she found him at his desk, looking like he was in deep thought.

He hadn't even noticed her standing against the door jamb, her arms folded across her chest. She decided to clear her throat, instead of knocking on the door, to get his attention.

"Eva, how long have you been standing there?"

Concern was etched in his face.

"Not long. You looked to be in deep thought, I didn't want to startle you."

"I'm fine, what are you doing up?"

She walked in, rounded his desk, and sat in his lap. She wrapped her arms around his neck.

"I rolled over and you weren't there, no nose whistle or anything. I got worried, so I looked for you in the one place you always go to, your office. And here you are. Is something wrong?"

He wrapped her up in his arms, and kissed her forehead. This, he could do forever.

"I just couldn't sleep. I'm having a hard time with all of this. On one hand, I want to lock you in the basement until all of this blows over. On the other hand, I'm not a caveman and I've never seen you so focused and hellbent on doing anything you can to help a friend. It's a double-edged sword. I want to keep you safe. But, if you insist on doing this your way, which you typically do, then I will do what I can to give you the tools you need to survive."

Tools to survive? What did that mean? She stared at the man who vowed to love her through thick and thin, sickness and health, for rich or for poor but, there was no mention of life or death situations, in snooping and murder investigating and hairbrain ideas.

"I don't know what to say. You know me better than I know myself. That whole lock me in the basement thing, well, I have ways around that. I know you're worried, hell I'm terrified but, I think this is the only way to end this."

"If you're terrified, why are you doing it? I need a good reason."

She had been musing over that exact thing the last day or so. She came up with one answer.

"I need to right a wrong. I tried to help my mom but I ended up killing her instead. I feel this will make up for it. I took a life, and now I'm trying to save one. Does that make sense?"

He hadn't seen that coming.

"I get it but, you're putting your own life at risk now, too. The kids and I couldn't make it, if something were to happen to you. Do you even know how much we love you?" He was pulling out all the stops, in the hopes that she'd change her mind. He knew he was playing dirty but he didn't care. She was his life.

Silent tears fell down her face, as her head slumped. Was she being selfish by doing something so dangerous and not thinking of the family she loved? He didn't give her time to respond, instead he put his index finger to her chin and lifted it slightly, and kissed her gently before she could say anything.

He knew it was no use trying to stop her anymore, this was something she had to do.

"It's okay Eva, I know you feel that this is some kind of calling for you, so I'm not going to object anymore.

I spoke with a friend of mine earlier, because I knew you weren't going to change your mind, no matter how hard I hoped.

He is sending me some equipment that should be here tomorrow. The tracking device is so small, and injectable, that it won't be detected. The wire will look like a small pair of earrings, but only one of them will have the actual wire in it."

"You did all that tonight, for me? I can't believe it. Who do you know that has access to that kind of stuff, anyway?"

"A friend from college and that's all I'm going to tell you." He stood up with her still attached to him.

She sensed the awkwardness in his voice, so she decided to drop the friend question, for now.

They both fell into bed, exhausted, mentally and emotionally. Eva didn't last but a couple minutes, before Kris heard the soft even breathing coming from her as she slept.

He laid awake thinking of all the possible scenarios that could go wrong with her plan. In the end, something in him told him she could very well make it work. It was that tiny little spark of hope that made him finally be able to fall asleep.

Chapter 35

Eva knew she was sleeping, and now dreaming. She came upon the same wooded area in Connecticut that she had been to in her previous dream.

Why was she suddenly dreaming of this place? It was definitely the same place, but a little different from the previous time. The trees were full of leaves, the temperature felt warmer, and the ground felt softer under her feet.

She made her way down the same path, wondering if she'd see her mother again. She hoped she would. But, after the last meeting, her mother had gone from sweet to angry in an instant. It was the dark magic that still lingered in her spirit. Eva knew there was still a white light in her soul, if she'd only be able to get her mom to acknowledge it.

She walked further into the wooded forest. She began to smell the familiar scent of burning wood, it was a campfire smell. She walked in the direction of the smell, knowing full well, this was where she was supposed to go. Her intuition telling her there was something waiting for her at the fire.

She stepped into the clearing, where she found a large bonfire burning brightly. It was there that she saw a figure sitting on the ground. It was shrouded in white, but she already knew it had to be her mother, waiting for her. Eva stepped closer, she was hesitating.

She stood in her spot, not saying a word, when she heard her mother speak.

"You can come closer dear, I'm not going to snap at you tonight."

Eva froze. She tried taking a step closer, but something wouldn't let her continue. Was it fear that made her hesitate like that or was another force keeping her from moving in closer? She didn't know. She gathered all her strength and took a slow step forward, then another. Her legs felt as if there were 30 lb. sand bags attached to her feet. She was moving so slow.

"He doesn't want you here. That's why your movements are hesitant."

Eva looked around at her surroundings. She was on high alert, and ready to dive behind the big oak tree if necessary, to protect herself from whoever her mother spoke of.

"He won't harm you dear, I won't let him. Please, continue dragging your feet over to me."

Eva approached her mother, dragging her feet with each step. She looked down and turned her head toward her so she could see her face, but her mother's straggly hair fell forward covering most of her face.

"Are you just going to stand there, or are you going to take a seat?"

Her mother had seemed to age since her last dream.

Eva didn't know what she wanted to do. She'd like to run like hell, back up the path that brought her here, and wake up from this weirdness. It was apparent that she was here for a purpose, and she was willing to find out what that purpose was.

"Why am I back here, Mom? Why do you keep bringing me here in my dreams? You have never tried to contact me since you passed, over twenty years ago, so why now?"

She wanted answers, but whether her mom would give them to her was another story. She waited, and nothing. Eva decided that if maybe she sat down, her mother might be more inclined to fill in the blanks.

"I haven't had a need to speak to you, until now. The moment you opened that spell book of mine, that's when I decided to seek you." She spoke with no real emotion in her hoarse voice.

"Seek me? What does that even mean? I opened the book, after all this time, to try to help a friend. I had vowed never to practice magic after that night. Until a few days ago, I kept that promise. As soon as this is over, I'm burning that book."

Her mother turned, and her eyes were piercing through Eva, they were as black as pitch. She remembered her mother having beautiful green eyes, the same eye color Eva had been blessed with, but the bright green was replaced with dark black, dead eyes There evil was in those eyes.

Eva scooted back a little, to put some distance between them.

Her mother laughed. "You'll never be as powerful as I was. You don't have it in you."

"I never wanted to be powerful, as you call it. I wanted a normal life, and that's what I had, until recently. Once this investigation is over, I'll go back to the way my life was before all of this nonsense started."

"Oh child, you have no idea what you have unleashed. He knows you have the gift. Now, he wants you, just as he wanted me."

She looked at her mother with furrowed brows. Eva asked, "Who are you talking about? Gerard?"

Her mother stood, gracefully moving around the fire. She was determining how to answer her daughter's question.

"Gerard? Is that what he is calling himself now? Interesting, I'd never pictured him as a Gerard. Anyway, remember the other night when I told you not everyone is as who they say they are?"

Eva thought back to her last dream and recalled her saying that, but didn't understand why.

"So what are you saying, he is the same evil entity that charmed you into the black magic?"

"You are smarter than I thought my dear. Yes he is. He is also the same energy that made it quite hard for you to move closer to me, yet you were to move and made your way to me. I'm starting to think that you are quite the conundrum for him, and he doesn't like it. You see, he always gets his way, nothing stops him, but you did. You are stronger than I gave you credit for; much stronger than I ever was. You may actually have a chance to have that normal life you so crave."

"Umm, thank you?"

Eva was clearly at a loss for words.

She stared at her mother for a minute. She could see how frail her frame was, even through the heavy white gown she was donning. Her mother didn't look strong at all, she looked weak. Eva was nothing like her. She was strong, not just physically, but mentally, too. She was much stronger and always one step ahead, where most people would have given up after seeing that scene on the fire escape. She had to know what happened and who could have done such a thing. Hence the reason she was in the position she was in now.

Eva had almost asked her mother for her opinion on her plan to be bait but, after seeing her and knowing that she was Gerard's puppet, she knew she couldn't tell her mother anything. And with that, she made her way towards her Mom, to say goodbye.

"It's been weird Mom, but I really need to be getting back. If there was nothing more you needed to say, I'll be leaving." Eva started walking to the path.

"Wait! Where do you think you're going? I'm not done talking to you." Alma's voice was shrill and echoed through the forest. Eva briefly stopped.

"I'm done talking to you mom. I've got my own life to live. I thought if I'd caught a glimpse of the white light in you that I saw the other night, I'd ask you to envelop yourself in it, because I'd known there'd be some good left in you. But now, I don't see it anywhere around you, so there is nothing more I can do."

Alma's head slumped slightly at her daughter's realization. It was a truth she knew, but tried hard to hide from her. She was hoping to get information out of her, for Gerard.

Her daughter really was smarter and stronger than she was. She'd let her go, even if it meant punishment for herself.

"I guess this is goodbye then," Alma said.

"Yes Mom, it is."

Eva started to walk down the path. Thunder rumbled, shaking the ground beneath her. She looked back to where her Mom still stood, and the fire rose higher, there were shapes forming in the flames. She started to go back to her Mom, when Alma yelled, "Go! Just go! I won't bring you back here, ever again. Now run!"

Eva saw the fire taking on the shape of the same creature that took her mother from her, that night so many years ago. She wanted so desperately to help her mother, to save her.

She started toward her, but her mother yelled once again, "I'm already dead, get the hell out of here! He can't hurt me anymore than he already has. Save yourself, please."

And with that, Eva ran faster than she'd ever run. She made it out of the forest, back to where she had started, and looked over her shoulder. There was a loud crack, and she noticed a white cloud of smoke rise up through the trees.

She turned back to where she had come from. She sat on the ground, knees bent, her head in her hands, and cried. She had lost her mother, again.

Eva felt hands on her. Someone was shaking her. She heard a faint voice talking to her, but it was muffled. Her arms flailed about, trying to get the person off of her. She felt soft lips touch her head, and a gentle whisper was trying to calm her.   There were strong arms trying to hold her. She didn't know where she was. Her eyes sprang open. Her vision was blurry at first, then the scene before her became clearer. She saw Kris, with a look of fear and worry on his face. She was home, and in her bed. The dream was over, she was safe.

"Eva you're okay. It was just a dream. Look at me, please." He was pleading with her.

"I'm home, in bed?"   She phrased it more like a question.

"Of course, where else would you be? That must have been some nightmare. Are you okay?"

She was still quite groggy and confused. She managed to sit up against the headboard, to get her bearings. She was safely home and in her bed, with her husband. Was she losing her mind? Was it really all just a dream? She honestly didn't think so. It was some kind of reality, she was sure of it.

As calmly as she could, she put her hand on Kris' face. "I'm sorry if I scared you. It really was quite a bad dream."

He looked down at her tenderly, but not quite believing that she was totally okay yet, not after what he'd woken up to. She was screaming, crying, and kept saying "I'd lost her again." He had never seen her like that before.

She started to get out of bed, when he stopped her.

"Where are you going?"

"It's 7am. I have to get the kids up and moving, and I have to get myself ready for work."

"You stay right where you are for a minute. I'll get the kids up." He leaned over, putting a kiss to her temple.

"I'm fine, really!" she yelled after him.

Chapter 36

Just as promised, Kris' package arrived via private courier before he even left for work. He took the box to his office, to open it. His friend did good. There was a tiny tracking device with a syringe that he'd sent with instructions, as well as a wire that looked like pearl earrings. Everything was traceable through Wi-Fi. He was impressed.

Still not liking Eva's idea of putting herself out there as bait, he tried to cover all his bases to ensure her safety. She knew how to shoot, and she carried her Bersa .380 with her all the time.

He made sure she was comfortable carrying a gun. He had her at the range every other weekend to practice.

Their kids were taught gun safety and have learned to shoot hunting rifles and small .22 caliber handguns. They both made sure their kids were aware of the dangers, and how to take precautions.

Kris didn't want their kids sheltered, especially in this day and age. He never sugarcoated anything. He wanted his kids to be vigilant and to think for themselves. And they did, much like their mother. He noted that both kids had her spirit, and strong willed attitude. He chuckled to himself.

He hadn't even heard Eva come into his office, until he looked up from his thoughts and saw her smiling at him.

"What's so entertaining," she asked.

He got up from his chair, walked around his desk, took her by the waist, and gave her a small peck on the cheek.

"You and our kids. I was just thinking how much they are both like you."

"Oh heavens. Let's hope they aren't exactly like me."

The box on Kris' desk caught her attention.

"What's in the box?"

He looked over his shoulder, as if he didn't know what she was talking about. "Oh, that's the equipment my friend sent me. It looks like good stuff.

Her stomach tightened. "You mean the tracking and wiring stuff?"

"Yes. Look at this wire. It looks like a normal pair of pearl earrings. And this tracking device... I inject it into your arm."

He was sounding a little more excited than she thought he'd be.

"You have to inject that thing into my arm? How do you get it back out?"

Her nerves were ramping up, and she knew she had to tamp them down, or he'd never let her go ahead with her plan.

Kris pulled the instructions from the box to show her. "You're not going to believe this but, after a month, the tracker dissolves. You don't have to worry about it being taken out."

"Wow, that is pretty ingenious. I like the earrings, too. They don't look like a wire, which I guess is the point, huh?"

Facing her, he sensed a hesitation in her voice.

"You don't have to do this you know."

She jerked her head around to face him. She tipped her chin up, her resolve was strong and unwavering. "This is not up for discussion, anymore. My mind is made up. This is the only way. We know they want to take me and this is probably the safest way. Besides, I just made plans with your parents to take the kids for a few days. Hopefully all of this will be over soon. Now, how and where do you need to inject this thing."

He knew there would be no further talk on the subject.

He took her hand in one of his, turning it over so the inside of her forearm was visible. He took the syringe in his other hand, and injected the tracker in the space between her wrist and her elbow.

"There, it's done. Now, I can log onto the site he included in the instructions, and I'll be able to track your every move for the next month."

She felt the tension rolling off him in waves. He was putting on a good front, but she could feel it.

"Awesome, so you'll know when I'm going to the bathroom for the next month," she joked.

He laughed. "Yeah, I guess I will."

All humor set aside, he pointed her to the couch, so they could talk.

"I want you to tell me your entire plan, and don't leave out anything you think is for my own good."

Ugh, of course he wants a laid out plan of attack. She was more of a fly by the seat of her pants, in the moment, lets see what happens kind of planner.

"Umm well, I was going to stay late at work tonight. If they see I'm still there, alone, it may draw them out. I'm counting on them thinking it'll be a good chance to snatch me."

She saw Kris' jaw clench, but continued on.

"If they end up falling for it, and take me, you would be able to track my every move. And with the wire, you'll hear everything, too. Once the tracker stops moving, you'll know where I am.   You could call Lt. Murphy and explain the situation, and give him the location. I'll do my best to get Gerard to admit that he killed Trudy. If I can do that, we'd have the proof we need to clear Chrissy."

Kris sat in silence, for what seemed like an eternity to Eva. He went to say something, then stopped himself, shook his head and looked her in the eyes.

"I admit, it's good and you've thought it out."
"But...?"

He took her hand in both of his, "but, what if we get to you too late? What if they just decide to..." he couldn't even say it out loud.

226

Eva filled it in for him. "What if they decide to just kill me, and be done with it?"

His eyes were glassy as he looked down at her. "Yes."

"If I tell you I have a few other things up my sleeve, would you feel better?" She tried for her trademark smile, but it hadn't quite reached her eyes.

"Do I even want to know?"

"Probably not, no."

He sighed in defeat. He pulled her into him and hugged her tight, not wanting to let go. He prayed this wouldn't be the last time he got to hold her like this.

She was thoroughly enjoying the warmth of his arms around her, and hearing the beating of his heart, which was faster than it should be. His breathing was steady though. She felt the fear he was holding in, and knew if she didn't go soon, she wouldn't go through with this.

She pulled herself back from the hug.

"I've got to get ready for work. Your parents are picking the kids up from school today, so you don't have to worry about watching for them after school.

"Okay."

That one word was all he could joke out before she left the room.

Chapter 37

Eva finished getting ready for work, and she made her way back down to the basement, to the wooden chest. She was in search of the brown wooden box that housed the sapphire ring that she had found the other day. She remembered something about it that looked off, but now she knew what it reminded her of.

She found it right where she had left it. She opened the box, took the ring out and held it up to the light. A white light bounced off the stone and covered her in a shroud of white.

"I knew it. It's a protection stone."

Eva had only heard of such a thing in her parents book of spells and witchcraft, but she had never actually seen one in person. She wasn't even sure if what it could supposedly do, was true. Now that she had one in her possession, she was positive she'd survive this.

"There's one of the things up my sleeve, or should I say, up my finger? No, that sounded stupid."

She was about finished getting ready for work, when her phone rang. She looked down at the screen, and saw that it was Chrissy's number.

"Hey Chrissy, I'm just on my way to work. Don't worry, I'll be there, soon."

"Well aren't you just the employee of the week."

Eva slid down the wall she was leaning against and sat there. "Who is this? Where's Chrisy?"

"Oh, she's hanging out with us for a little while."

"I want to talk to her, now."

"You are a feisty little thing, aren't you? Quite like your mother."

Eva froze. "What did you say?"

"Your mother, she was very fiesty, if I remember correctly. But, she knew her place and knew not to mess with me."

It took Eva a minute to process what she was hearing. She remembered her mother saying something about Gerard in her dream, but how did she... "You took my mother! You charmed her over to the dark side of magic. It was you."

"Now, now Eva. She honestly didn't need much convincing. She wanted the power, and she was addicted to it. Now, I want you. If you do as I say, your friend will live. But if you don't, well you can blame yourself for what happens to her."

"You will never make me change over to dark magic, or any magic for that reason. You're wasting your time on me, if that's what you want. I don't do magic and haven't since you killed my mother. Now, what is it you want me to do?"

"You're lying Eva. I know you've practiced magic, in the last few days to be exact. But that discussion can wait till later. And by the way, it was you who had killed your mother, isn't that right?

Eva thought she would throw up. He was right, she had killed her mother.

"Eva, are you still with me?"

She croaked out a whispered yes.

"Good. Now, I will need you to come to the warehouse that stands to the left of the airport, on Pittsburgh Drive. Alone Eva, and don't tip anyone off, or I'll know."

"Wait! I want to hear Chrissy's voice, to know she's okay, then I'll leave."

She heard some talking in the background. There were more than two people there. She also heard what sounded like chair legs scraping across the floor. It was so high pitched, it made Eva pull the phone from her ear.

It went silent for a second, then she heard a groan, and then Chrissy's voice. It was shaky. "Eva?"

"Chrissy! Are you okay? Are you hurt?"

"I don't know where I am. The only voice I recognize is Gerard."

A sudden scuffling noise and a scream cut into Eva's heart. "Chrissy! Chrissy!"

"You've heard her, now get over here, now. I'm done talking." *Click*

She stood in the middle of her kitchen, paralyzed. Eva hoped to God Kris was either hearing or at least recording this. He wouldn't have gotten the other side of the conversation, but he'd get the gist surely.

She snapped herself out of the shock she was drifting in and out of, so she could think straight. She did a double check of herself. "

Wired earrings... check. Tracker in my arm... check. And Grandma Lilly's sapphire ring... check.

She went in search of her keys, and purse, then she bent to her ankle and patted the side of it where she was now carrying her .380.

"Let's hope they don't look there."

Opening the garage, she peeked out and looked up and down the street. She wanted to see if anything looked out of place. She didn't notice anything different, but that didn't mean anything. She was feeling jumpy, and just wanted to get in her car.

She sat in her car, and waited for her phone to connect to her bluetooth. Once it was connected, she turned on Pandora. She thought better when she was listening to her music. It was amazing how music could calm her brain enough to think.

Out of the corner of her eye she saw a piece of paper on the passenger seat. She picked it up, opened it, and it was a note from Kris.

"Oh God, what is this about," she protested.

But as she read the short note, her eyes stung with tears.

Eva,

I just wanted you to know how proud I am of you, and how you never give up. I wanted to tell you earlier, but I couldn't get it out. Please know that I love you more than anything on this planet, and I always will, forever. Be safe, and know that I can always hear you, as long as you have those earrings on. I will be listening, and the moment I see on the tracker that you have left the house, I'll know where you are at all times.

I love you, Always and Forever,

Kris

SHe wiped the tears from her face, folded the note, and put it in her purse. So many emotions flitted through her. She gathered herself, and took steadying breaths. She was about to put her car in reverse, when her phone went off again, but this time it was a text.

Eva, what are you waiting for? Time is ticking…

"Shit!"

Was he watching for her to leave? She shoved the gear into reverse, backed out of the driveway, and sped down the street.

She was halfway to the airpark, when Kris tried calling, but she let it go to voicemail. She figured that he noticed she wasn't going the way she would go, if she was going to work. He must be tracking her now. Which meant he was probably listening, too.

"If you can hear me, I'm not going into work, as you probably noticed. Gerard has Chrissy, and told me to go to the warehouse on the left side of the airport, off of Pittsburgh Drive. One way or another, this is going to end today. He said he'd know if I went to the cops, so he probably has someone following me. Once you hear anything after I'm in, pay attention to whether or not I get him to admit to Trudy's murder. Once you hear that, send Murphy and his calvary in. And Kris, I read your note, thank you. I love you, always and forever, too."

*****

"Damn it Eva!"

Kris swore at his computer, where he had started watching the tracker. When he heard her talking to, who he assumed was Gerard, he hadn't stopped listening to her. He decided to check the tracker then too. He knew something was wrong.

He balled his fists tight. He felt helpless, and wanted to go after her. That would be the normal thing to do. With his head in his hands, he prayed.

Chapter 38

Eva drove the fifteen minute drive to the airpark. The main street, Houk Rd. was lined with warehouses and airplane hangars. Most were still up and running, but a few had been abandoned over the years.

The runways were straight ahead on Pittsburgh Drive. The Delaware Municipal airport was used mostly for smaller aircraft, like Beechcraft Bonanzas' or King Air private jets, and some planes that were a little bigger, like puddle jumpers. There were no large Airbus Jumbo jets that could land here.

The only warehouse near the airport was a dilapidated hangar that hadn't been used in, what looked like thirty years or more.

"This has to be the place he was talking about."

As she pulled into the area, she could see the cracks in the asphalt and the weeds growing up in between them. What were once windows in the hangar, were now pieces of leftover glass or plexiglass. The metal forming the building was rusting and holes from that rusty were showing its damage.

She stopped her car close to a door that led inside. Before she got out, she started talking to herself, but she knew she was talking to her lifeline, her husband.

"I am at the location, which is not a warehouse. It's an old rusted out airplane hangar. Here goes nothing. And Kris, I love you."

WIth her mental checklist, she examined all the places on her body that held every piece of protection that she had. Silently praying it would all be enough.

******

He heard her every word, and had recorded everything.

"Let's get this over with Eva. You're going to come home to me tonight," he guaranteed.

******

She walked towards the door, and stopped when she heard a noise. It was a chair being dragged, she thought. She opened the door, which made the most hideous sound she'd ever heard. It was worse than fingernails going down a chalkboard. *So much for a stealth approach.*

It was dark and dingy looking inside. Dust motes were floating through the air, and spider webs hung from everywhere.

Her phone started to buzz in her pocket, which made her jump.

"Jesus Christ, what the hell?"

Looking at the text that had just come in. It was from Shannon, wondering where she was.

"Shit! I don't have time for this."

"I'll take the phone Mrs. St.Claire." A foreign female voice came out of the darkness.

Eva turned in a full circle, trying to locate the voice. Heels clicked on the cement floor, coming closer, and she continued whipping her head from side to side trying to locate the threat.

She came waltzing out from behind a large plane engine that had been forgotten about years ago. The female approached her like a lioness targeting her prey. She was tall, skinny, with longish brown hair perfectly coiffed, her makeup was flawless on her alabaster skin, and her golden eyes sparkled with evil.

It was Gemma, but a more dangerous looking Gemma.

"Gemma? Where is Chrissy?"

"Hand over the phone Eva, and I'll let you see her."

Eva did as asked, and gave her the phone. Gemma pocketed the phone, and grabbed Eva's arm. She turned her so she was up against a dirty wall. Gemma started patting her down, obviously looking for weapons.

My gun. She's going to take it. Probably shoot me with it, too.

237

Eva's thoughts were all over the place. She hadn't thought about getting pat down.

"Well, what do we have here? Little Miss Eva carries a gun."

"Yes, what's your point? You found it, now let me see Chrissy."

Gemma turned Eva back around so she was facing her, and pushed her back up against the wall, and spit in her face.

"You don't give me orders, I give the orders, remember that, if you want to live," she growled.

Eva went silent. She was thanking her lucky stars she hadn't taken the earrings, or her sapphire ring. She hoped to God Kris was hearing all of this.

Gemma wrapped a hand tight around Eva's upper arm, and she yanked her deeper into the hangar. It was bigger inside than she expected.

"Where are we going," Eva squealed.

"Someone wants to see you."

They had rounded a corner where she could see a built in office. It was inside the hangar. She shoved Eva through the open door. Eva tripped and fell to the ground. She quickly got to her feet. As she looked around the space, she immediately saw Chrissy. She was tied to a chair, gagged and her head slumped forward. She noticed blood dripping from the corner of her mouth. Eva about threw up. She bent down to her friend, shaking her slightly. She was trying to wake her up, but she didn't even flinch.

"What did you do to her?"

"She'll recover." A male voice came smoothly from behind her.

Eva whirled around and came face to face with Gerard. He was smiling down at her. His smile was anything but pleasant.

If he wasn't such an evil bastard, he might be handsome, she thought. He was bordering on six feet, had olive skin, thick waves of brown hair with touches of silver at the temple, and a muscular upper body that narrowed at the waist. His face is what Eva stared at. He bore at least two or three days' worth of growth on his beard, he sported a perfect set of white teeth, but his eyes were the same pitch black she saw in her mother.

She steeled herself back a few feet, to put some space between them.

"Let her go. I'm here now. You said she would be let go if I came."

He stood in the doorway, his arms folded over his chest. He scoffed at her, "she can hardly leave now, she's not even conscious."

Eva knew that. "How long will she be out? What did you drug her with?"

He walked into the office, and purposely brushed against Eva's shoulder. His touch made her jerk away. He leaned against the large metal desk that took up forty percent of the office, and stayed silent for a minute.

He looked down at Chrissy, smirking. "She has a little while yet before she'll be coming to. It will give us time to, how should I put this… get to know each other better, Eva."

Repulsed by his comment, Eva was growing more and more disgusted with this man, and what he had done. Not just to Chrissy, but to Trudy, too.

"I don't want to get to know you better. I want to get her out of here, and away from you, as soon as I can."

He stared at her with his black eyes, hoping to make her crack. She could feel his intentions. She also knew she needed to keep him talking.

"Gerard, one thing I want to know," she hedged.

He looked almost entertained that she was attempting to have a conversation with him.

"What is it you want to know, Eva?"

"What is the real reason you killed Trudy Marshall?"

Her face remained void of emotion. She wanted his answer, then Kris could contact Lt. Murphy, and they could get this over with.

A maniacal laugh came out of him. It didn't look or sound normal. He stood, hands on his hips, and took two steps toward her, then stopped.

She could see the wheels turning through his expression. He wanted to hurt her, she could see that. But, she also saw that she could be valuable to him, just like her mother was supposed to be, until Eva stopped her and ended her life. The flames in his eyes, were the same flames that formed his real identity.

She was unconsciously stroking the sapphire ring that was on her right ring finger.

****

Kris was on the edge of his seat, waiting, and listening, for anything that they could be used as evidence of Trudy's murder. He knew they could obviously get him for kidnapping, but Eva made his swear to her, not to call Murphy until he heard him admit to the murder. *Stubborn woman.*

He continued listening. He didn't like the way she was egging him. He didn't think this Gerard was all that stable to begin with.

Finally giving into his own fear for his wife, he used his office phone to call Lt. Murphy. She could be mad at him all she wanted. He was going to get the man to come to his office, and then they would both listen in. He could even send his men into the area, so they were ready to engage.

Lt. Murphy picked up on the second ring. After Kris explained the situation, in length, he thought the man might arrest him. But the man agreed to come to his office. Luckily for Kris, his office was downtown as well, so he figured he'd be here fairly soon.

****

Gerard's sister Gemma was growing bored with the conversation, and got into Eva's face.

"Listen little one, you should be very afraid, my brother isn't the only one who can tear you into tiny little pieces. I don't care the least bit about you."

"Gemma! Stand down."

She whipped her head toward her brother, her teeth bared, and eyes wild. "We're wasting time, just get on with it then."

Eva looked between the siblings, wondering what that meant. What *"get on with it"* meant.

He stepped in front of his sister, grabbed her jaw with a strong hand, and made her squeal.

242

"This is my show, not yours. You failed the last time, so I must do everything myself."

He held her gaze for a second, then he slammed his lips to hers, in a deep, angry kiss.

Eva felt a wave of nausea roll over her. They were siblings, she thought.

The moment calmed briefly, as Gemma took her place as the underling, but continued to give Eva the death stare.

Eva heard a door shut out in the main part of the hangar, then footsteps sounded like they were coming closer. Eva turned to look toward the office door, and saw Jack Walker standing there. There was no emotion in his face. He looked dead inside.

"Jack, why are you here?"

He continued to stare at her, no expression formed on his face. He didn't answer her, he just looked to Gerard for some silent conversation, she wasn't privy to.

"Hello!?"

Before she knew it, Jack backhanded her in the face, and she fell to the ground, holding her cheek. She checked for any bleeding. Her cheek hurt, and tears burned her eyes. She gritted her teeth and held them back.

"What the hell was that for," she yelled.

Gerard squatted down in front of her.

"Looks to me, like you pissed him off," he said, chuckling.

She looked up at Jack and noticed his eyes were the same black as Gerards. That wasn't good.

Eva knew some witches had the power to take over a person's body, and they were basically zombified and had no idea what they were doing. Apparently Gerard was one of those witches, she thought.

"How come he got to hit her and I couldn't," Gemma piped up.

"You'll get your turn to have fun with her, I promise." He winked at his sister.

"Nobody needs to play, or hit anyone, thank you very much." Eva tried to make that very clear.

They looked at each other, clearly enjoying their new toy, and they loved watching her squirm.

"Okay, you two are clearly having a private moment at my expense, but I am growing tired of it, can we move on. You still haven't answered my question, Gerard," she asserted.

"She's got a temper," Gemma quipped.

"That she does. I think I like it."

Gerard touched the spot on her cheek that still burned.

Eva slapped his hand away. He quickly put her in a choke hold, and it was starting to cut off her air supply. She flailed, scratching and kicking, but he was stronger.

He had his mouth to her ear, and whispered, "do you want to end up like Trudy? I could do it so quickly, from top to bottom in mere seconds. You wouldn't know what hit you. Too bad I don't have my shears with me."

****

"My god, that guy is seriously demented," the lieutenant said. He was listening to everything going on in the hangar. "I'm calling in my guys to storm the place."

"You heard him talking about how he would do the same thing to Eva as he did to Trudy. Chrissy is obviously innocent."

"Yes, I heard everything. You're saving all of this aren't you?"

"Absolutely."

Something brought them both back to listening.

****

"Darling, I've got your shears with me."

Everyone looked up from where they were. Eva had nearly fainted.

"Mother, what a nice surprise. What are you doing here?"

Gerard stood, and walked to where his mother stood. She was a petite woman, with silver hair that hung straight to the top of her shoulder. She had pale complexion, but neary a wrinkle on her youthful face. She dressed in clothes typically meant for attending brunch at the country club. Her gray pant suit was flattering, with her black Prada pumps. She was holding a box that Eva recognized.

Her son gave her a kiss on her cheek and stepped back, to accept the box she'd brought.

"I'm not sure I'll be needing those, Mother. You see Eva here, is the daughter of Alma. You remember Alma, don't you?"

She looked toward Eva, and smiled. "So you're Alma's spawn. I wish I could say that it was a pleasure to meet you, but your mother became quite a problem for my son."

Eva's mind was spinning out of control. She'd never got anything about his mother being part of this. She was so confused. She thought it could have been the hit from Jack that knocked something loose, but she didn't know.

"My mother has been dead for over twenty years. Why is this an issue, now?"

"My son wanted her, and she agreed to be part of him, to make him stronger, and more powerful. But, you took that away when you killed her."

Still confused, Eva tried to stand and regain some sort of stance.

"Okay, but what did that have to do with Trudy and framing Chrissy?"

Eva looked down at Chrissy, and she thought she could see some movement, but she ignored it.

The matriarch was now sitting behind the desk, giving the impression that she was really the boss here. She steepled her fingers together, as she leaned back in the desk chair. She focused her attention on Eva and her question.

"Nothing. It was just one way we figured we could get to you dear."

Eva's jaw dropped at the older woman's statement. Realizing that this whole thing was all a ruse, just to get to her. She felt sick.

******

Kris was having a heart attack, as he was listening in.

"Now! Get her out of there now," he growled.

Murphy was already on the horn, calling in SWAT and anyone else available.

"Mr. St.Claire, I have to go. We will get your wife and her boss out of there, as soon as possible. But, I need you to stay here."

"I'm not staying here. I'm going with you." He started to stand.

Lt. Murphy held his hand up. "I can't let you go. Please stay here, until I contact you. Don't make me arrest you sir."

He flopped back into his seat. Kris felt the life draining from him by the second. He figured he would wait five minutes, then he'd take off.

He continued listening. He was cracking his knuckles, grinding his teeth and losing his mind.

"They were after my wife this whole time. Why?"

******

Still numb from the realization that she was the center of this whole disaster, Eva touched the sapphire. She was thinking of her grandma Lilly, and her mom. They were so different. Eva always thought she was more like her grandma, not her mother. These people wouldn't want her. She didn't have an evil bone in her body.

She saw movement out of her peripheral vision and it made her look up. She saw that Chrissy was coming around. She scooted herself over to her friend, taking her hand.

"Chrissy, wake up," she encouraged.

"Step away from her," Alice said, jerking up from her chair.

"I just want to make sure she's okay."

"She'll be fine. She may be a little pissed once she finds out that all of this was your fault, but she'll be fine otherwise."

The office was lined with enemies. All of whom wanted to harm her, and didn't care if she lived or died. She had never known the three, that were hell bent on destroying her, all because of her mother. She swore under her breath, "even dead, you're still doing damage."

"What did you say," Gerard asked.

"I was talking to myself."

"Eva? Is that you," Chrissy groaned through the gag on her mouth.

She went to go kneel next to her friend, but her leg was swept out from under her so quickly, she hadn't seen it coming. She fell hard onto her knee, and let out a whimper from the pain that was radiating through her leg.

The next thing she sees is her own gun pointed at her head. It was being held by Jack. She shrank back into herself, not ready to die just yet.

Chrissy was becoming more and more aware of her surroundings, and the horror showed on her face, as she saw the gun pointed at Eva.

Chrissy tried wiggling her way out of the ties that they had bound her in, but they were too tight. She tried to speak through the gag, but it was muffled.

"Leave her alone." Chrissy was attempting to say.

With the gun now suddenly pointed at her, her eyes were as big as saucers. Alice stepped up to where Chrissy sat, and pulled out the still bloody shears. She cut her ties, and withdrew the gag. Chrissy rubbed her wrists and flexed her jaw, but remained quiet.

"You can go sit with your friend now." Alice directed her to where Eva was sitting.

She dropped to the floor next Eva, and pulled her in for a hug.

"Oh God Eva, are you okay," she cried.

She held onto her friend, and shook her head, unable to talk.

"Now what are we going to do with them," Gemma asked. She looked all too excited at the prospects.

Eva heard a faint noise out in the hangar, and prayed to God it was the cops. She hoped Kris had heard everything and called Lt. Murphy. Her face remained void of emotion. She didn't want to let on that she'd heard anything. She had a plan if bullets were going to start flying. She started mindlessly stroking the sapphire again.

"Yes Gerard, what are you wanting to do with these two? I'm getting bored," his mother said.

"I'm hoping Eva will agree to join me, as her mother had intended to do," he said sweetly.

Eva felt pure revulsion towards the man in front of her.

"I'd say you really don't have a choice Eva. You do as I ask, or you both die. Hmmm...I guess you do have a choice, in a way." He laughed.

Chrissy sat sobbing next to her. Eva's ears were still honed in on the very slight noises she was starting to hear. They were coming closer, and she was surprised they couldn't hear it.

Jack stood there like a statue, not paying any attention to anything. He looked like he was in a trance.

Gemma was seated in the desk chair that her mother had vacated, and Alice was playing with her phone. The only one paying any kind of attention was Gerard, and his soul focus was on Eva. He was waiting for her to answer.

"So what's it going to be Eva? Me or death?"

"Neither."

"That's quite disappointing Eva. We would be perfect together, as one very powerful witch. I know what you can do. I've seen it, and I saw you in the clearing. You were able to dream travel, and you got a picture of Gemma in the car. You never would have been able to do that without some superior magical skills."

She took the time he was talking, to slip off the sapphire ring. She held it tightly in her right hand, and felt the light cover drape over her and Chrissy. She was glad that they had put her down here with her. It was much easier to protect her, as well.

Gerard was so engrossed with his own words, he hadn't even seen her do anything.

He took the gun that Jack had been holding, and pointed it directly at Eva and Chrissy.

Eva noticed the red dot on Gerard's forehead, and knew that he wasn't going to have the chance to use it.

Gemma saw it, too and sat up quickly, yelling, "Gerard, get down!"

Everything seemed to happen all at once, in a cloud of chaos. Shots rang out, and everyone but Jack hit the ground.

Gerard pointed the gun directly at Eva's chest and pulled the trigger. The bullet ricocheted right off of her, and their protection shield. His face went slack, and he took off running, followed by his sister and mother. Jack was left standing in his comatose state.

Eva and Chrissy sat on the floor huddled together, while a series of gunshots rang out in the main hangar.

They could hear orders being shouted over the noise. Then an eerie silence came over the place.

A couple officers appeared in the doorway of the office, where the girls remained together.

After she heard everything go silent, Eva had thought ahead, and had put the sapphire ring back on her finger, releasing the shroud of protection.

One of the officers bent down to check on them, and told them that the paramedics were on their way. Another officer was handcuffing Jack as he was coming out of his trancelike state. He was in a complete loss of time and space. He didn't know where he was, or what had just happened, only that he was now being arrested.

Eva drew up the courage to ask the officers, "what happened to the others?"

The officer was thoughtful for a moment, while he tried to decide how to answer her question. He phrased it as gently as he could.

"They are deceased, ma'am."

Eva's head dropped into her hands, and tears streamed down her face. The officer put his hand on her shoulder, trying to comfort her, but there wasn't anything that could calm her at this point.

The medics came running through the door, with their gear in hand. They attended to Chrissy, who was in shock, and not speaking.

"Ma'am, are you hurt anywhere else besides this cut on your mouth?"

She didn't answer them, she just stared off into space.

Eva pulled her head out of her hands. "They may have drugged her. She was unconscious when I got here."

Chrissy looked at Eva, still not speaking.

"We're going to take her to the hospital and get her checked out thoroughly."

They loaded her on a stretcher and wheeled her out.

Eva sank farther to the floor, and watched as another medic came in to check her out.

She heard yelling in the hangar, and the familiar voice perked her up. It was Kris.

"My husband, he's out there, I can hear him. Please, let him in here. I need to see him." She was begging them. The medic stood and went to fetch him.

Eva sent up a silent prayer in thanks, to God and her Grandma Lilly for saving her. And to her husband, for helping her, and bringing the cops in when they did.

"Eva!"

She held her arms out for him. He dropped to the ground and pulled her into his lap, hugging her tightly. He didn't think he was ever going to let her go. Tears threatened, as he felt her warmth and could see that she was safe.

She pulled back a little to see his face. She was surprised it was wet from his own tears. She wiped his face gently with her hand.

"Thanks for sending in the cavalry when you did." She smiled at him.

"You're bleeding.

She put her hand to her cheek, where she'd been hit. It hadn't been bleeding before.

"I don't think it's my blood. I was holding Chrissy close to me, and she had a cut near her mouth, I think it's hers."

Relief flooded through him, but he could see the beginning of a large bruise forming on the side of her face, and he frowned.

She saw the look on his face. "I'm fine. It could have been a lot worse. I will probably have a nice goose egg on my knee, too, but other than that, I'm good. Let's get out of here."

They both looked to the medics, and they gave them a nod.

He helped her up from the floor. He took her hand, and felt something on her finger. He pulled up her hand to see the sapphire ring she was wearing. He had never seen it before.

With a questioning look on his face, Eva explained to him what it was and what it had done. She then told him where she had found it.

WIth a sweet smile on his face, he continued walking toward the exit, holding onto her hand. "Thank you Grandma Lilly!" he proclaimed.

Chapter 39

A few days had passed since the unfortunate events. Everything was starting to get back to normal. Chrissy and Eva both, had taken a few days off to recover.

Chrissy had gotten checked out at the hospital. They had found remnants of GHB in her system, which explained why she'd been unconscious when Eva had found her. She still couldn't remember how, or where they had grabbed her though.

Jack was sitting in jail, now. They found out that Gerard had blackmailed him into helping him, by threatening to expose his other lifestyle.

Gerard's mother, Alice had heard what Trudy had done to Jack and Emma's marriage. She had mentioned it to Gerard, in passing. He figured he wouldn't mind helping him with his scheme. If he refused, Gerard would expose him. He told the police he didn't have a choice. Unfortunately, Jack didn't remember anything from the day in the hangar.

He will still be charged with accessory to kidnap, murder and indentity theft.

Eva felt horrible for Emma and her kids.

She and Kris had spent a couple of days while the kids were with their grandparents, resting and talking to Lt. Murphy about the events that had unfolded. Kris gave the lieutenant all the recordings from the wire, and he assured them that all charges had been dropped against Chrissy.

To Eva's surprise, the man never did mention a word about what he'd subsequently heard, regarding her being a witch. She was truly grateful for that.

Both Chrissy and Eva had fielded many calls from the girls they worked with. They had been checking on them constantly. None of them could believe what had happened in their little town.

The local news had been all over it, trying to get the women to do interviews. They both declined.

The day after Chrissy had gotten out of the hospital, she had called Eva to check on her. She also asked her about how the bullet had ricocheted off her, when clearly she saw it going right to her chest. Chrissy wasn't sure if she had seen it correctly, or if it had been the drugs in her system that had made her see the bullet bounce off of them.

Eva didn't want to lie, but she didn't want to have to explain her past anymore than she already had, so she told her it had to have been the drugs. Chrissy seemed satisfied with her answer, so she dropped the subject.

It was going to take them both a while to get over what had happened to them in that hangar. They both had good support systems in their families. And for that, they were thankful.

Eva still couldn't fully relax. She thought, yes, they said the three were deceased, but if the other two were anything like Gerard, only the physical body that they had inhabited was dead. Their evil spirit was probably still out there, searching for their next host.

Chapter 40

Eva was napping on the couch when she heard the doorbell. Kris was in the kitchen when she heard him walking to the door to answer it.

A man's voice carried to her, one she didn't recognize. She sat up and headed to the door where her husband was standing, shaking hands with a gentleman she had never seen before.

"Hello." she said, sleepily.

"Eva, I thought you were sleeping."

"I was, until I heard the doorbell."

The man looked apologetic.

"I'm so sorry I woke you."

He held out his hand to her. "I'm Jake Long, a friend of your husband's, from college."

It took Eva a second to process, but she put two and two together. "The earrings and the tracker." She stated, matter of factly.

He shook his head in acknowledgment. "Yes, those were from me."

"Those things saved my life. I can't thank you enough for getting them to Kris so quickly."

"Anything for a friend. I'm just happy you're okay."

"I'm getting there," she whispered. She clasped her husband's hand in hers.

"I was wondering if I'd be able to have a word with my friend here," he asked.

Eva perked up, getting the gist that she was interrupting. "Oh gosh, of course, I'm sorry. I was just going to go get a shower. I'll leave you two to talk."

She gave Kris a quick hug before heading up the stairs.

Kris invited his friend into the den, where they would be able to relax and chat.

"Nice house St.Claire."

"Thanks Jake. Now, what are you really doing here?"

"You can read me a book dude, always could, even in school."

"Yeah, it's a real talent."

Kris knew Jake had something up his sleeve. His anxiety meter had jumped ten points.

Sitting across from his college roommate, Jake saw how happy his friend was, with the life he chose. He envied him.

Jake was an eternal bachelor, because his job didn't allow for much else. Sure, he had adrenaline rushes now and then, and the occasional life flashing before your eyes. Working as a field agent with the FBI did that to a person.

Kris was losing patience waiting for the man to drop the hammer, and get on with whatever he'd come here to say.

"Jake, talk to me."

"Alright, alright… the thing is, you're not the only one who heard everything that went on that day."

He stopped talking, letting his words sink into Kris' head. Kris' eyes widened slightly. "Who else heard the transmission?"

"I was listening in. Don't get mad. After you called me the other day, I got worried that you were in trouble, so before I packaged the stuff up to send you, I formatted the wire so I could get a WiFi link to it, as well."

Kris stood up quickly. He was pacing, and wanted to punch the guy in the throat, but thought better of it.

"Okay, so you heard everything. What does that mean?"

"It means, I may be interested in you and your wife doing some work for me, at the FBI."

Eva's lower jaw about hit the floor where she'd been standing outside the den.   She had stealthy made her way back downstairs. Her curiosity had peaked and

262

wondered about this friend of Kris'. So, being nosey beat out the hot shower.

Now, she stood stock still, and stunned.

"FBI? Me and Kris working with the FBI," she thought.

Then realization hit her like a brick.

They want to use me, for my magic…

The End

Thank you for reading A Killer Cut. I hope you enjoyed reading it, as much as I did writing it. It looks as though Eva isn't quite finished with her magical past just yet.

Stay tuned for her and her husband Kris' next adventure.

Made in the USA
Monee, IL
29 August 2020